Praise for

The Winemaker Detective

Twenty-two books
A hit on television in France

"The perfect mystery to read with a glass of vino in hand."

—*Shelf Awareness* starred review

"Will whet appetites of fans of both *Iron Chef* and *Murder, She Wrote*."

—*Booklist*

"Unusually adept at description, the authors manage to paint everything.... The journey through its pages is not to be rushed."

—*ForeWord Reviews*

"I love good mysteries. I love good wine. So imagine my joy at finding a great mystery about wine, and winemaking, and the whole culture of that fascinating world. And then I find it's the first of a series. I can see myself enjoying many a bottle of wine while enjoying the adventures of Benjamin Cooker in this terrific new series."

—William Martin, *New York Times* bestselling author

Deadly

Tasting

A Winemaker Detective Mystery

Jean-Pierre Alaux
and
Noël Balen

Translated from French by Sally Pane

LE FRENCH BOOK █

First published in France as
Saint Pétrus et le saigneur
by Jean-Pierre Alaux and Noël Balen

World copyright ©Librairie Arthème Fayard, 2005

English translation copyright ©2014 Sally Pane

First published in English in 2014
By Le French Book, Inc., New York

http://www.lefrenchbook.com

Translation by Sally Pane
Copyediting by Amy Richards
Cover designed by David Zampa
Proofreading by Chris Gage

ISBNs:
Trade paperback: 9781939474216
Ebook: 9781939474209
Hardback: 9781939474223

Let beer be for those who are perishing,
wine for those who are in anguish!

Let them drink and forget their poverty
and remember their misery no more.

Book of Proverbs, 31:6-7

1

Drinking unsweetened Darjeeling tea was not a problem. Resisting the three crispy little biscuits taunting him from the white porcelain dish was another thing. The evening before, his wife had told him the time had come to shed the extra pounds that were making his shirts gape between the buttons. Benjamin Cooker had, indeed, filled out a bit over the past few months. He preferred to think that his heavy neck and chin, full cheeks, prominent belly, and belt hooked in the first notch gave him the look of a bon vivant, a well-off and satisfied man in his fifties.

Elisabeth Cooker, however, did not agree. The extra weight wasn't good for his looks or his health, so she had taken matters into her own hands. She had gotten hold of a cabbage soup diet purportedly prescribed by the cardiology department of a large urban hospital for obese patients who needed to lose weight before surgery. Elizabeth had cut a large head of cabbage, four slivers of garlic, six large onions, a dozen peeled tomatoes, six carrots, two green peppers, and one stalk of celery and plunged them into three quarts of water with three cubes of fat-free chicken broth. The mixture, seasoned with salt, pepper, curry powder, and parsley, had been boiled for ten minutes and then simmered until all the vegetables were tender. Benjamin was supposed to eat this soup whenever he was hungry over the course of seven days. It was not meant to be the only source of nourishment, and to avoid nutritional deficiencies, he would be allowed fruits, additional vegetables, rice, milk, or a piece of red meat, depending on the day.

The first day promised to be especially grueling. Other than the soup, fruit was all that Benjamin was permitted. And that was limited. He couldn't have any bananas. Benjamin surmised they were too tasty for this Spartan regimen. For drinks he could have only unsweetened tea, natural fruit juice, and water. The wine expert had initially rebelled, citing his professional obligations, upcoming wine tastings, and business lunches. Elisabeth had responded by giving one of his love handles an affectionate pinch. Surrendering, he had leaned over her and planted a grumpy kiss in the hollow of her neck.

There were only a few patrons on the terrace of the Café Régent in downtown Bordeaux, and the damp morning foreshadowed the first chill of fall. Benjamin drank his scalding-hot tea, reached for the small white dish without looking at the perfectly golden crust on the biscuits, and offered it to the person at the next table: an elderly lady with hair pulled back in a bun who was attentively reading the last pages of the local daily newspaper, the *Sud-Ouest,* which contained the weather forecast and the horoscopes. She thanked him and gobbled the pastries in three quick bites. He stood, nodded good-bye, and resolutely took off toward the Allées de Tourny.

He was about to climb the large staircase to his office when a digital toccata rang out from the cell phone deep inside the pocket of his Loden. He dug the device out, pressed the answer button, and Inspector Barbaroux's gravelly voice assaulted his eardrum. Getting straight to the point without so much as a greeting, the police inspector asked Benjamin to come immediately to 8B Rue Maucoudinat. The detective had a clipped, authoritative tone, perhaps to give away as little information as possible. Irritated, Benjamin made a quick about-face and headed for the Saint Pierre neighborhood. He was not in the habit of complying so swiftly, and he was almost angry with himself for doing what the captain wanted without getting any explanation.

Arriving at the Place Camille Jullian, Benjamin spotted two police cars blocking the narrow street, their doors wide open and lights flashing. An ambulance was parked nearby. The street had also been cordoned off. A uniformed officer recognized Benjamin from afar and unhooked the crime-scene tape to let him pass. He explained that the captain was waiting for him on the third floor of the small building at the corner of the Rue des Trois Chandeliers. Other police officers were holding back a crowd of onlookers, many of whom were standing on their toes to catch a glimpse of whatever was happening behind the flowerpots on the balcony. Benjamin rushed up the two flights of wooden stairs without so much as holding onto the railing and made his way down the hall, where two plainclothes detectives were talking with a woman in a white coat. They all turned and looked him up and down without a word.

"Hello," Benjamin panted. "I believe the inspector is expecting me."

"I don't know if he can be disturbed," said one of the men. "Access to the area is prohibited."

"This way, Mr. Cooker," Barbaroux bellowed from inside the apartment.

In the hallway, an empty gurney sat next to an umbrella stand, which was also empty. The wallpaper, with tedious rows of droopy floral bouquets, oozed a musty odor. Faded prints of religious scenes, shepherds on the heath, and dove hunters added little charm to the stuffy dark tunnel that opened onto a cramped living room furnished in birch veneer.

"Sorry to trouble you, but I needed to see you right away," the inspector said, his hands stuffed into the pockets of his trousers. "Thanks for coming so quickly."

"What happened?" Benjamin asked, overlooking the fact that Barbaroux hadn't bothered to shake his hand. "It must be serious if you've blocked the road off."

"Everyone says you're the most brilliant wine expert of your generation," Barbaroux said. "Some even claim that you're one of the best in the world. Is that true?"

"You didn't bring me here to shower me with compliments, I hope."

"Don't think I'm being sarcastic, Mr. Cooker. That's not my style. But it happens that I need your expertise right now."

The woman in the white coat came into the room. Her hand was raised, and she appeared to be asking permission to cut the conversation short. Two morgue attendants wearing serious expressions were standing behind her.

"My team has finished, Chief. Can we remove the body now?"

"You haven't forgotten anything?" Barbaroux growled.

"Everything's ready to go. We have what we need."

"What about those samples we rushed to the lab?"

"You should be getting the results any minute now."

"In that case, get him out of here!"

The men pushed the gurney through a door that Benjamin had not noticed before, leaving it open as they attempted to lift the half-naked and bloody body. It took several tries, and at one point they almost dropped the corpse. The wine expert averted his eyes and made a sign of the cross.

"Jules-Ernest Grémillon, ninety-three years old," said Barbaroux. "Not a bad age to die."

"Are you going to tell me what happened in this apartment or not?"

"Do you really want to know?" he asked, looking Cooker in the eye. "Well then, follow me."

They went into the kitchen, which looked hardly bigger than a few square feet. The floor, laminate counter, and wall tiles were splattered with dark stains that looked nearly black, except where the dim ceiling light reflected ruby red spots. Cooker felt his stomach lurch, and he was grateful there wasn't much in it. He frowned.

"Total carnage!" Barbaroux said. "The old man was butchered like a pig. What a mess! According to preliminary findings, the victim tried to defend himself before he was struck. It looks like the killer attacked quickly. Over there, the clean dishes on the drain board fell onto the dirty dishes in the sink. They're all smashed. And there, the pans were knocked off the hooks. A box of macaroni is spilled all over the floor."

Benjamin looked on without a word, trying to control the revulsion he felt in this ravaged, bloodstained kitchen, a repugnant cesspool where the most barbaric violence had mixed with the ordinary misery of everyday life.

"But the strangest thing, Mr. Cooker, is behind you," the inspector said, touching the winemaker lightly on the shoulder. "Turn around. I want you to see this. Odd, isn't it?"

On a small wooden table wedged behind the door, right beside the refrigerator, a dozen wine glasses were arranged in a semicircle. Only one, the glass on the extreme right, was full.

"What's the meaning of that?" Benjamin asked, dumbfounded.

"Well, exactly, it's incomprehensible! We're all shocked, I have to admit. This neat little scene in the midst of bloody chaos. Obviously, the murderer took his sweet time leaving a calling card. But what's the message?"

"And what's in the glass?"

"Don't worry. It's not the victim's blood. I'm sure it's just red wine. We sent a sample to the lab. We've taken all the photos and measurements we need. We've dusted for fingerprints, tested everything—absolutely everything—under UV light. Now all I need is you."

"And how can I be of use?"

"Other than you, I don't know anyone who can tell me what is in this glass."

"You're kidding, Inspector. You want me to do a blind tasting on the spot, at the scene of the crime, amid this slaughter?"

"I suppose these are not ideal conditions, but you would be doing me a great favor."

"I'm sorry, Inspector. I would like to help you. But how do we know that what's in the glass, which looks like wine, hasn't been tainted? You can't ask me to taste it without giving me some assurance that there's nothing in it that could make me sick."

"As I said, we sent a sample to the lab, and they're rushing a tox screen. I'll know in a minute or two."

Benjamin didn't have enough time to refuse the detective's request. Barbaroux's cell phone rang. The inspector pulled it out, put it to his ear, and mumbled a few words before ending the call and tucking the device back into his pocket.

"That was the lab. Quick, aren't they? It's wine, and the tox screen didn't reveal anything worrisome. You can go ahead and do your tasting."

Benjamin sighed. There was no way out. He picked up the glass and tipped it carefully to observe the color, search for particles, and examine the density of the surface reflection. Then he brought the glass to his nose and closed his eyes. There was dead silence, barely interrupted by a slight swishing sound when the wine finally rolled into Benjamin's mouth. He savored it slowly, taking some air into his throat before letting the wine slide to the back of his mouth. He spit the wine onto the dish shards in the sink. Then he began all over, his eyes still half-closed, as the inspector watched. Benjamin sensed the man's impatience but still took his time, employing the same expert approach, the same palpitating nostrils, lip movements, and slow, almost lazy chewing, punctuated with wet and noisy clicks.

"Well?" Barbaroux asked, unable to conceal his impatience any longer.

"Astonishing!"

"Where's it from?"

"A very nice nose! Delicate, generous, balanced!"

"Where's it from?"

"On the palate, it's a bit disappointing."

"But where's it from?"

"The aromas are elegant, but the mouthfeel is somewhat faded."

"You don't know?"

"Time has softened the structure."

"And where's it from?"

"Pomerol."

"Without a doubt?"

"Without a doubt."

"And what else?"

"Let me see..."

"What estate?"

"I have an idea what it might be."

"So tell me, for God's sake!"

"I can never be sure, but..."

"But?"

"Pétrus."

"Are you sure?"

"Almost sure... Yes, absolutely."

"Almost or absolutely?"

"Both."

"What year?"

"You're asking too much."

"More or less?"

"An old vintage."

"Approximately how old?"

"It could be sixty years old. Possibly even older."

"Really? You don't say! Still, you're not being very precise."

"Sorry."

"Any memory of it?"

"I never tasted it before."

2

"Oh no, sir, you're not too heavy!"

"Come now, Virgile, don't flatter me. You don't need to be polite."

"Maybe a little chubby. That's all."

"In any case, I've never been svelte. I get that from my grandfather Eugene. All the Frontenac men are built like rugby players. It's in the genes."

"Well, on a frame like yours, the weight is fine. You just have that kind of build."

"Yet, on the English side they are all a bit lean and even rather thin. My brother looks like a Cooker, but my father is the best example of that lineage."

"I've never had the honor of meeting him."

"He's very distinguished and elegant. Elisabeth finds him very classy."

"Your wife probably put you on a diet to prevent future health problems."

"That's right. Take her side! Why don't you just go ahead and say I'm fat. You'll sound just like her."

"I didn't mean to suggest anything, sir. I'm just trying to imagine what made her prescribe this little diet for you."

"You must be kidding, boy. A little diet? I had to cancel an important luncheon appointment today. Instead of having a nice meal with a colleague, I'll be choking down my nasty ration of cabbage soup, which will supposedly work miracles by the end of the week."

"How do you mean?"

"Elisabeth's goal is to have me lose ten pounds and no less!"

"Oh, that's very doable, sir," Virgile said.

Benjamin was getting irritated with Virgile, who was being entirely too cheerful and supportive of this god-awful eating plan. Sometimes it was better to just keep your mouth shut. But Benjamin could see that his annoyance was having an effect on his fiercely loyal assistant, and he immediately regretted his peevishness.

He got up from his swivel chair and smiled at the young man. "You're right, my boy. It's certainly very doable. In any case, I've never been able to say no to my wife." Benjamin sighed. Of course, she had only the best of intentions, and he loved her for wanting to take good care of him. "Come, follow me!"

They walked to the small place at the end of the hall that served as kitchen, storeroom, and library for Cooker & Co.

"Look what Jacqueline bought us."

"Your secretary has gotten us a microwave?"

"I suspect Elisabeth had her buy it for us." The Cooker & Co. office had a certain Second Empire patina that was becoming increasingly hard for Benjamin to maintain. The copy machine, computers, and wireless router were rude intrusions. And now there was a microwave.

"For *us*, you say? Do you mean I am involved in this, too?"

"To tell the truth, Virgile, I don't know how to work this machine. And I have no intention of polarizing any of my molecules while I'm heating up this damned soup."

"It's not very complicated," Virgile said, reaching for the plastic container next to the microwave.

He lifted the lid, stirred the vegetables floating on top of the broth, sniffed the mixture, and turned to his boss with a broad smile.

"This cabbage soup doesn't look bad at all! And if you don't mind, I'd be happy to share it with you."

"You'd do that for me, Virgile? You'd share this ordeal with me?"

"Why not?"

"In that case, be my guest."

They returned to Benjamin's office with their steaming bowls of soup. And as they sipped, they began organizing the tasting program they needed to finish by the end of the following week. Benjamin was counting on Virgile to help him elaborate on his impressions and confirm his notes so that he could perfect his chapter on Languedoc-Roussillon wines for the next edition of the *Cooker Guide*. The Fitou, Minervois, Saint-Chinian, Faugères, and Cabardès appellations, as well as all the Quatorze, La Clape, Picpoul de Pinet, Cabrières, Saturnin, Montpeyroux, Saint-Drézéry, Saint-Georges-d'Orques, and Pic-Saint-Loup estates had already been completed, but they still had much to do.

New samples awaited them in the laboratory directed by Alexandrine de la Palussière on the Avenue Chapeau Rouge. Benjamin knew she was having an increasingly difficult time figuring out how to store, classify, and prepare the tasting sessions. The rooms were at capacity, and the incessant deliveries were filling every nook and cranny, often hindering personnel and slowing the analyses for Cooker & Co. clients. Such was the price of success, and Benjamin was aware that sooner or later he would have to enlarge the space to accommodate the numerous wineries that were clamoring for his services and advice.

They had to keep up a good pace to complete the tastings, especially the Corbières and clairettes of Languedoc and Bellegarde, not to mention the Méjanelle, Vérargues, Saint-Christol, and Malepère slopes. Faced with the magnitude of the task, Benjamin had decided to postpone some assessments of the naturally sweet wines, especially the Maury, Banyuls, Rivesaltes, and muscats of Lunel, Mireval, Frontignan, and Saint-Jean-de-Minervois.

"I'm afraid we won't be able to get it all done in two weeks," Virgile said, blowing on his spoon before taking another sip of soup.

"It's a matter of organization. We will work in segments. No more than thirty wines at a time, and I think we can reach our goal in three or four sessions per day."

"You're an optimist, sir. Personally, I am saturated after fifty."

"That happens to me, too. That's why I need your help. Besides, it's one of the benefits of working as a team."

"Of course."

"You don't look convinced. But you know very well that if the two of us work together, we can get ten times as much done."

"You have a funny way of doing math, boss. I'd say we can do at least twice as much, which is pretty good."

"No, I disagree, Virgile. I've often observed that we've increased production tenfold when we've worked as a team. It may not be logical, but the record speaks for itself."

The telephone rang. Benjamin put aside his theories, his professorial air, and his bowl of soup and reached for the receiver with a scowl—another interruption that could keep them from getting their work done. As he put the receiver to his ear, he watched Virgile plunge his spoon back into the soup and fish out the last morsels of vegetables. He listened to the caller in utter disbelief, mumbled good-bye, and hung up.

"Nothing serious, I hope?" asked Virgile.

"Something god-awful. Something really sick and disgusting."

Such trite words weren't Benjamin's usual vernacular. He was more likely to use a more formal phrase, perhaps "something horrendous," or "quite despicable," or "nauseating." Benjamin could tell his assistant was alarmed. With good reason. He had just gotten some really god-awful news.

§ § §

On their way to the Place du Parlement, Benjamin told Virgile about the Jules-Ernest Grémillon murder, the carnage in the kitchen at the Rue Maucoudinat apartment, and the glass of Pétrus found in the middle of the mysterious and macabre display. Walking briskly, he shared every last detail with his assistant. Although winded, he was even able to keep a few steps ahead of the younger man.

"Why didn't you tell me sooner, Mr. Cooker?"

"Why should I worry you? Besides, you always accuse me of sticking my nose in places where it doesn't belong."

"But this is different. They came looking for you. And if that was Barbaroux who just called, I bet there must be more trouble."

"Good guess, my boy."

Benjamin, followed by Virgile, broke into a jog. The Rue du Chai des Farines, a long and narrow street flanked by the dark facades of tall buildings, most of them dating from the eighteenth century, was filled with police cars, their lights flashing. Once again, there was an ambulance, and crime-scene tape was stretched across the sidewalks to keep curious onlookers out. Benjamin had the feeling of déjà vu.

He recognized the police officer who had let him in that morning and gave him a nod to indicate he was not alone. Virgile flashed the officer one of his charming smiles, and Benjamin and he went through the barricade without needing to identify themselves. They passed under a carriage entrance and crossed the mossy cobblestones of an interior courtyard to the double entry doors, which stood open.

Inside, the forensics team had not finished taking fingerprints, and Inspector Barbaroux greeted them in a hushed voice. He asked them not to touch anything. An old man was lying in a pool of blood on an oriental rug. His cheek was crushed, and his bathrobe had been slashed open at the shoulders and abdomen. Swelling flesh and blood were oozing from the wounds and already congealing on the woolen fibers of the robe. The victim was barefoot, and his toenails were curled upward, like inverted talons of a bird of prey. His sheepskin slippers had ended up near the polished Henry II table, which gleamed under the yellowish light of a hanging porcelain lamp. Twelve wineglasses had been carefully arranged in a semicircle. Two of them, on the right side, were filled with what Benjamin supposed was red wine.

"We've already sent the samples to the lab, and they're clean. I will ask you to repeat what you did this morning," the inspector murmured.

"Who is it?" Benjamin asked.

"Émile Chaussagne, eighty-eight years old. That's all I know."

Benjamin and Virgile looked away while the morgue attendants picked up the corpse and slid it onto the gurney. A photographer took some final shots of the room. Inspector Barbaroux asked Benjamin to approach the table.

"You know what you need to do, don't you?"

Benjamin was quick and tasted the two glasses without excessive ritual. He swirled the glasses three times each to gauge the body. He captured

the aromas with his nose and took two small
chewing sips with his eyes closed. He trusted his
memory and remembered exactly all the nuances
he had identified in his previous tasting.

"I covered the essentials this morning, and I
don't have much to add," he said, turning to his
assistant. "Virgile, would you like to give us your
impressions?"

"No thanks, sir."

"I thought you were more adventurous,"
Benjamin said with a touch of sarcasm. "Does it
have anything to do with the effect our lunch is
having on your stomach?"

"You've got that right, boss."

"You're feeling the cabbage?"

"There's a war going on in my belly. How
about yours?"

Barbaroux cleared his throat. Benjamin
guessed he wanted to cut the conversation short.
The inspector seemed a bit nervous, too. The
coins he was jingling in his trouser pockets were
the giveaway.

"Is it Pétrus again?" he asked brusquely.

"I think so."

"The same one as before?"

"I would guess it is. At any rate, it's the same
vintage."

"What about the bottle?"

"What do you mean?"

"Is this Pétrus from the same bottle?"

"It's impossible to answer that question. I'm not a psychic."

"With you, one never knows."

"I know an African witch doctor in the Saint Michel neighborhood. You should try him!"

"Don't mess with me, Mr. Cooker. This is serious, and for the moment we're not leaving the Saint Pierre neighborhood."

"I wasn't suggesting that we all pay him a visit. I just thought you might be interested. At any rate, if I'm not mistaken, you're thinking that the choice of wine wasn't coincidental."

"Yes, there may be a link between where the murders occurred—the Saint Pierre neighborhood—and these glasses of wine—Saint Pétrus."

"That may be. But it seems to be a very expensive calling card. There has to be more to this. Why announce each murder with wine and such an exceptional vintage at that?"

"That's the real question," Barbaroux conceded. "We also need to know why the murderer lined up his twelve glasses that way. I'd put money on the number being significant."

"Surely the number twelve is important," Benjamin agreed, scratching his head. "It is often said that this number symbolizes the cyclical nature of the universe, and you find it in many civilizations and rituals: the twelve apostles at the Last Supper, the twelve gates of Jerusalem, the twelve signs of the zodiac, the twelve lost tribes of

Israel, the twelve fruits from the tree of life, and so on."

"*The Magnificent Twelve*," Virgile threw in.

"No, it's *The Magnificent Seven*, my boy. Yul Brynner. It was based on *Seven Samurai*. A classic. Rent it sometime."

"Oh yes, that's right, I always confuse it with *Snow White and the Seven Dwarfs*."

Benjamin sighed and raised his eyes to heaven. Sometimes it was impossible to follow Virgile's thinking, and there were occasions when he didn't even want to. He looked at the inspector. "We digress. I am convinced that the number is even more important because it indicates a sequence of events. I think the murderer intends to strike twelve times, since he fills a new glass with each murder."

"I'm sure of it. He's telling us that there will be ten more crimes, and all of them will be the same. There's no doubt about it."

"He won't let up until all twelve glasses are full," Benjamin agreed.

"He must have an impressive wine cellar if he intends to keep using Pétrus."

"It's not so much the market value of the bottles that intrigues me, but rather the vintage. This is definitely an old wine and therefore rare, even hard to find. And why this one in particular?"

"The number twelve, this particular wine, the setting: they appear to be symbolic and connected," the inspector said as he started to leave.

"I'm thinking the same thing. Also, the victims are all more or less the same age. That's certainly an element to consider in this investigation."

"Let me do my job, Mr. Cooker. I know very well what I need to investigate and how to proceed."

"Of course, Inspector. But be careful when you accuse me of meddling in your business. I didn't just show up and volunteer. You dragged me into this."

"I would be out of line to accuse you of volunteering for this assignment," the inspector agreed. "Let's try to work together as best we can—that is, if you're intrigued by the case. I only ask that you keep me informed of anything you happen to find out."

"Certainly. I'm going to see a friend who can give me more information."

"May I have this friend's name?"

"I'd rather not divulge it at this point."

"Whatever you think is best," said Barbaroux. He thrust out his chin without taking his hands out of his pockets. Benjamin returned the detective's wordless good-bye with a nod.

Benjamin, followed by a silent Virgile, stepped out of the apartment. His stomach was bloated and gassy. Elisabeth had warned him the first few days of the diet might be slightly embarrassing. He had also been advised not to smoke, but he reached for his sharkskin cigar case and took out a magnificent Cohiba Siglo VI, whose cap seemed especially supple. He lit the Cuban cigar with relish and drew several generous puffs of the honeyed flavors. He held the smoke in his mouth as long as possible, allowing it to temporarily satisfy his hunger.

3

Ensconced in his convertible, Benjamin had been waiting for more than half an hour when he finally saw Franck Dubourdieu through the vapor on his windshield. His friend, dressed simply in white shorts and a navy T-shirt, was whistling as he emerged from the tennis club. He had a terrycloth was draped around his neck and a gym bag slung over his shoulder. He was carrying a racket.

"Hey, Benjamin!" he yelled, seeing the winemaker. "What are you doing here?"

Benjamin climbed out of his classic Mercedes 280 SL and almost winced when Franck shook his hand with the forceful grip typical of exuberant athletes.

"I thought I might catch you here when I didn't find you at home."

"As always, Benjamin, you know how to follow your nose. I'm getting a later-than-usual start today. But as you're aware, I usually try to squeeze in a game of tennis before I get down to work."

"Did you win, at least?"

"Win or lose, who cares? The key with age is to keep improving, like good wine. Hopefully, the wine is thoroughly relished and gone before it has the chance to turn into vinegar."

Franck Dubourdieu's house was a stone's throw from the Primrose Tennis Club, one of the posh spots in the city, always a fashionable place to go when you wanted to hit a few balls in polite company. In this well-manicured and slightly snobbish neighborhood called Caudran, Franck maintained an unaffected attitude without prejudice or concerns about social status. He was focused only on enjoying life. As an agronomist, trained oenologist, and, above all, a long-standing friend, he often surprised Benjamin with his appreciation of poetry, his integrity in tasting innumerable crus, and the equal delight he took in a Beethoven quartet and a Chet Baker ballad. His sense of youthfulness and wonder was still intact, and this trait never failed to charm Benjamin.

"If you don't mind, I'll take a quick shower," Franck said as he opened the door to his home and threw his bag in the entryway. "I'll just be ten minutes. In the meantime, taste this 1989 Suduiraut-Cuvée-Madame. It's a beauty."

He uncorked a bottle, put two crystal glasses on the coffee table in the living room, and left Benjamin with his glass of dessert wine. He disappeared upstairs, but not before taking time to slide a Lennie Tristano CD into the stereo.

The pianist's harmonic progressions swept up and down the keys. The melody rose in torrents before cascading in fine dulcet droplets that made Al Levitt's cymbals tremble delicately. The melody ascended again, driven this time by the smooth, sustained sounds of Lee Konitz's alto saxophone and the supple modulation of tenor Warne Marsh. Benjamin found himself pleasantly carried away, and he instinctively felt the intensity and depth of Tristano's genius.

Unlike Franck, who was an aficionado, Benjamin had never immersed himself in the world of jazz. He found it a bit intimidating, and yet it had analogies in the world of wine. While the jazz lover deciphered the liner notes on an album, the wine connoisseur gleaned information from the label on a bottle. The jazz lover eagerly committed to memory the names of hundreds—perhaps thousands—of artists and could surmise which were shooting stars and which were eternal flames. Similarly, the wine connoisseur could commit to memory myriad domains with mysterious names. The jazz lover noted innovative creative trends the same way a wine lover discovered emerging terroirs. And listening, feeling, and analyzing a rhythmic meter or harmonic thread were similar to tasting, feeling, and analyzing an aromatic palate or tannic presence. Indeed, there were many palpable connections between jazz and wine.

"Ah, 1952, a great vintage," Franck said as he pulled on an old cashmere sweater. "The July 17 concert in Toronto. Peter Ind on contrabass and Al Levitt on drums. Tight section, very smooth, with just the right amount of tension. I like this album because the pieces are long, as they often are on stage, and it's the duration that brings out the best in this music. It's got beautiful development—firm and fluid, full of finesse. Complex but elegant: it has aged majestically, believe me!"

Benjamin raised his glass of Sauternes and nodded in agreement with his friend's remarks, affecting an air of competence that he did not actually have. He admired Franck's work in oenology and often consulted his books on the topic, especially *Les Grands Bordeaux*, published by Mollat. He kept a worn copy on his writing table.

"Do you know that Elisabeth is infatuated with genealogy, etymology, and heraldry and has done some research on your name?"

"Really? How is your charming wife?"

"Very well, thank you. She found a certain Bernard Dubourdieu, who was a brilliant captain under Napoleon. If my memory serves me, he was born in 1773 and died in 1811. He took part in campaigns in Italy and Egypt, distinguishing himself in numerous battles against the British Navy. In short, he was one hell of a character. But the strangest thing is that he was the son of a master cooper from Bayonne. It seems that if your name is Dubourdieu, you are destined to be involved in the wine world."

"Surprising, indeed. But I don't think he was one of my ancestors. As far as I know, anyway."

"Four years before he died in artillery fire in the Mediterranean, he sailed to Bordeaux on a ship called *La Pénélope*. Records show he captured thirteen British vessels, including two privateers, and took three hundred prisoners."

"That's interesting, Benjamin, and please thank Elisabeth for looking into the subject, but I don't imagine that you came all this way to tell me the story of this particular Dubourdieu, who had the luck to be born in a wine barrel and gave up the ghost at sea."

Benjamin sipped the Suduiraut and clicked his tongue.

"You are right, Franck. I just need you to give me your insights on Pomerol."

"I don't know what I could possibly teach you," Dubourdieu said. "You know perfectly well what I think of you, and I get some rather caustic comments from jealous colleagues when I tell them. But hey, you're heads and shoulders above the rest of us, and you have to accept that."

"It's nice of you to think so," mumbled Benjamin, who always felt embarrassed at being so highly regarded. "But I think you, on the contrary, could help me in a rather delicate matter. Let's say it's a sensitive case."

"I don't like it when you get that worried look on your face."

"Have you had a chance to watch the news today?"

"No, I haven't had the time. You forget that I just played three hard sets against a formidable opponent."

"There were two slayings in the Saint Pierre neighborhood a couple of hours apart. Two men well over eighty. A ritual appears to be involved in both, although I don't think the police have told the reporters about that yet."

"How were they killed?"

"Knifed. Both of the men were stabbed and bled like pigs. But for me, the most intriguing part of these two cases is the wine that was left at the scenes. Twelve glasses were lined up in both apartments. At the first, one glass was filled, and at the second, two glasses were filled."

Benjamin relayed the information meticulously, detailing every point, including the fact that he had tasted the wine at each murder scene.

"You're really sure it's a Pomerol?" Franck asked with a frown. He got up from the couch to turn down the music.

"Yes, absolutely certain. I let the inspector believe I was hesitating, but I have no doubt. On the other hand, I'm completely stuck as to the vintage."

"You must have a suspicion, though."

"To be honest, all I know is that it is not very young and that I've never tasted it before. But I don't want to tell you any more. The inspector gave me two samples, and I have the test tubes in my pocket."

"I imagine all this must remain confidential."

"Obviously. I trust your opinion as much as your discretion."

"Thank you, Benjamin. I'm happy to be of any help, but don't be too optimistic. You know as well as I do that it's a tricky business."

Franck Dubourdieu brought out two new glasses and set them on the coffee table. Benjamin poured out the contents of the test tubes and waited patiently for his friend to begin tasting. From the corner of his eye he watched Dubourdieu weigh, observe, sniff, and chew the wine in his own personal style.

Lennie Tristano continued his melodic forays, and Lee Konitz and Warne Marsh responded with their own. It was all brotherly jousting, where the point wasn't winning or losing, but savoring the camaraderie.

"I have an idea, and I'm surprised you didn't tell me about it," Franck said right away.

"That is?" Benjamin said slyly.

"It's a Pétrus, and you knew it. You couldn't possibly have missed it."

"That's exactly right. But admit that it was tempting not to let on ahead of time. It's part of the game."

"I don't blame you. I would have done the same thing. That said, this is not an exceptional year. It is, indeed, a very old vintage, but it's the nose that lets you perceive the characteristics of Pétrus. The body is a bit weakened, and I suspect we are dealing with an average harvest."

"If you are being so careful, you must have a clue."

"It does remind me of certain very distinctive years in the Bordeaux region."

On the stereo, the blending of ivory, ebony, and brass with just the right amount of genius, reverie, tension, and sweat culminated in a moment of grace. The music went silent. Dubourdieu put the CD back in its case and slipped it into a cabinet drawer under the letter *T*, between Cecil Taylor and McCoy Tyner.

"I have the feeling that this wine could be well more than a half century old," Dubourdieu continued as he started looking through another drawer of CDs.

"Okay, so what?"

"It could be from the nineteen forties. You must have thought of that too."

"Yes, the oldest Pétrus I have ever tasted was from 1945. We all know that was a remarkable year. We call it the vintage of the century, mostly because it's closely linked to the end of World War Two in Europe. I admit it's one of my most spectacular wine tasting memories."

"I've also tasted it, and I agree with you."

"I have had many chances to taste post-war Pétrus, and even though those specimens were superb, they couldn't quite match the 1945."

"You've never tasted the ones produced during the war?" Dubourdieu asked. He took out a CD of the Gerry Mulligan Quartet recorded in 1952 on the Pacific Jazz label.

"No, I haven't."

"Those wines have the same iconic bouquet. But the mouthfeel is light. Maybe that's a clue. I would opt for a 1943, but you'd have to check by opening one from the same vintage."

"Why 1943?"

"Because it's a good year but not a spectacular one. Mind you, Pétrus is a remarkable wine, regardless of the year. Nevertheless, winemakers throughout the Bordeaux region faced terrible obstacles during the war. The men were off fighting, and the women and children had to tend the vineyards and make the wine, on top of what they were already doing. Most of them weren't as experienced as the men. In addition, all equipment and trucks had been requisitioned for the war effort, and that slowed harvests and production. Those who were left on the estates managed pretty well and were even quite valiant, but the quality of the wine was affected."

"You really believe this is a vintage from that period?" Benjamin asked.

"It's entirely possible, but to get a more precise idea, we would have to find bottles from that vintage, assuming they are still well-preserved and drinkable."

Gerry Mulligan's baritone sax was rising above the trumpet sounds of Chet Baker. The ringtone of Benjamin's cell phone was a shrill interruption. He stepped into the hallway to take the call and returned to the living room a few minutes later.

"Is something wrong, Benjamin?"

"That was Inspector Barbaroux. There's more trouble."

4

A harpsichord piece by Scarlatti, a Jamaican calypso, a soft-drink commercial, an old Celine Dion hit, an urgent news flash, a Muslim sermon, some nineteen sixties rubbish, a futile discussion of euthanasia... Benjamin impatiently scanned the radio stations on his car radio. He stopped when he recognized the familiar voice of Rudolph Martinez. Benjamin had been invited to the France Bleu Gironde radio studio each time a new edition of his guide was released. He had come to know this mysterious young man with elegant hands and a dark, seductive gaze beneath long eyelashes. Benjamin appreciated the interviewer's pertinent and carefully researched questions. The engaging dialogue always made for a successful show.

Benjamin slowed down and turned up the volume; he loved the incisive clarity of Martinez's commentaries. This one was mischievously titled "Bobo of Bordeaux":

Bordeaux suffers from a pernicious type of modesty that keeps us from proclaiming our superiority. Let me explain: on the radio or television, how many times have you heard people say, "No, Bordeaux is not cold" or "No, Bordeaux is not dreary"? In print, how many times have you seen Bordeaux described as a sleeping beauty—a young woman who's hardly even alive? Even our mayor has gone on the defensive, saying that Bordeaux is not the stiff and stuffy city that certain people say it is. Why are we always denying our vibrancy and flagellating ourselves? In truth, under Bordeaux's gray eye shadow, there's a passionate young woman who's just waiting. She's wearing red lip gloss and a lacy thong. She's funny, festive, and sexy. She just needs to be stirred a bit.

Benjamin parked on a grassy embankment and turned off the engine. Martinez's slightly naughty and understated humor put him in a good mood. He turned up the volume, unable to suppress a gleeful smile that made his reflection look a bit silly in the rearview mirror.

We all know that Bordeaux is not fond of change. When she's not described as a sleeping beauty, she's considered aloof, her bosom held firmly in a corset. That makes her safe and respectable. But safe and respectable are for other cities, not our fine and bedazzling Bordeaux. The young woman from the Garonne is ready to toss away her chastity belt and be emancipated! Enough of the sad and disturbing stuff of the past. Today's Bordeaux is a rare beauty ready to seduce both those who live here and those fortunate enough to visit.

A Spanish truck whizzed by. It brushed dangerously close to the convertible, and the displaced air shook the car. Benjamin turned the volume up even more.

The people of Bordeaux must go off the defensive and take charge of the future. Our city, this sleeping beauty, just needs to be kissed by the prince. And *voilà*. We have the city we dreamed of. Those who write and talk about this city need to get with it. Continuing to call Bordeaux cold, boring, lethargic, nostalgic, distant, aloof, and sleepy just makes me grumpy and sleepy. I realize I'm mixing my fairy tales, but you understand what I'm saying.

"Well said, kid!" Benjamin exclaimed as he restarted the engine.

It was, in fact, time to put those clichés to rest. The city had changed considerably since the time, now ancient, when the writer Francois

Mauriac had fled the sorrows of his childhood, the suffocating secrets of his family, the Sunday rituals, and the Jansenist smell of the Grand-Lebrun high school to be reborn in the lights of Paris. Benjamin remembered a little book written in the nineteen twenties in which Mauriac had described Bordeaux as "endlessly organized in a hierarchy." The road a resident lived on, the type of wine he sold, and other more subtle distinctions classified him as ship owner or merchant, wine trader or fishmonger.

Still, Benjamin realized that some of those observations were still relevant, especially if you spent any time in the Chartrons neighborhood: "In Bordeaux, the gap between pretense and reality shocks you at first. Then it makes you laugh"; "Bordeaux is the port city that makes you dream of the ocean, but the ocean is never seen or heard."

Benjamin continued on his way, savoring Martinez's iconoclastic—to say the least—program, which nonchalantly wandered from syrupy violin pieces, Mississippi bluesmen, and Brazilian cooing to funky horn selections, London rock, and Byzantine choirs. This guy had a sense of connection and tempo and a depth of musical knowledge that allowed him to tweak his listeners with just the right amount of bad taste to keep them both intrigued and amused.

As he approached Libourne, road construction slowed traffic. He turned off and headed toward the first street that seemed clear. Trusting a vague sense of orientation, Benjamin made several detours in an area with tidy houses whose white plastic fences vainly attempted to imitate lacquered wood. After turning into two dead-ends and finding himself in the same traffic circle a number of times, he arrived on the road that led to the cemetery. A police van and two unmarked cars were parked outside the main entrance. A plainclothes detective stood guard on a carpet of wet grass. The winemaker identified himself and was allowed to enter. He could make out the slightly compact, oblique profile of Inspector Barbaroux, who was gesticulating in the middle of a small group of people.

Benjamin walked down the first road and cut through a row of vaults, some of which, surrounded by rusty gates or decorated with small stylized chapels, were in need of weeding.

Benjamin saw Barbaroux wave to him and start to walk over. The inspector extended his hand when he reached Benjamin. It was sweaty. He's still on edge, Benjamin thought.

"Thank you for coming so quickly," Barbaroux grumbled as they started walking toward the spot where the inspector had been talking to the group of people. "But you didn't need to. I could have sent the samples to your office."

"Your phone call made me too curious. I had to come. What happened, exactly?" They had reached the grave site, and Benjamin nodded to the three experts from the forensics unit who were standing on its perimeter.

The tombstone was coldly austere and clearly desecrated. But Benjamin could still make out the name on the black marble plaque in the middle. It read:

ARMAND JOUVENAZE

1914–1998

The final *e* of the name had been covered with a thick *i* of red paint that had dripped before drying just above the date. The concrete cross overlooking the burial place hung dismally by the end of its metal structure.

"Look at this shit," the inspector said. "Someone took a sledgehammer to the headstone and that slanderous transformation of his name. And, as usual, the fucking twelve glasses."

"Three of them filled," Benjamin said, approaching the grave. "Except this time, the body has been aged!"

Barbaroux gave a hint of a smile and then broke into a full grin. "More than a decade fermenting in the cellar!"

"He was a contemporary of the first two victims."

"That's worth noting. We've locked down the area, photographed the grave site, and taken samples from the glasses. If you feel like tasting them, they're all yours."

Benjamin proceeded fairly quickly, crouching near the grave and spitting the wine on the grass. He carefully set down each of the three glasses.

"These are not ideal conditions, but I can confirm what I told you the two previous times."

"Pétrus?"

"Yes, the wine is a bit too cold. Although it's not that chilly outside for October, the wine has been sitting here for several hours, which has compromised it somewhat. I can't tell you much more."

Barbaroux motioned to his forensics team to clear out. He told them to wait for him at the cemetery entrance. Then he turned back to Benjamin, who was examining the red paint. "That slur painted there smells of vengeance," he said, pulling a tissue from his coat pocket just in time to catch a sneeze.

"You're right. It seems like a fairly straightforward message to me. Maybe a bit cartoonish, but hey, obviously this Armand Jouvenaze was lucky to die when he did, or else he might have been butchered like the two others. Why he is being called a Nazi, well, that's certainly a lead to pursue."

Barbaroux wiped a drop from the end of his nose and stared at the winemaker. There were dark circles under his tired eyes.

"You're a shrewd one, Mr. Cooker."

"Why do you say that?"

"In Lot-et-Garonne, where I come from, we would even say you're a *sacré mariole*—which means pretty clever, and a bit of a smart-ass."

"Is that so?"

"You've put your finger on the only really interesting point. Clearly, this desecration is connected to the two murders. But from the beginning, we've assumed that the person doing this might be planning twelve murders. It seems now that there won't necessarily be twelve victims."

"I agree with you," Benjamin said, "Some of the people who've been targeted might already be deceased. Just consider the ages of the two men who were slain and the man in this grave."

"That's what I mean about being clever!"

"It all seems very logical. Our challenge is finding out why these men have been targeted."

"Yes, it's useful to know what drives the perpetrator of a crime. It usually has to do with passion, whether it's hatred or love, vengeance or remorse."

"So you have to find out if this Jouvenaze has a past, and why he's being called a Nazi. I'm sure you've already looked into the backgrounds of the two victims, right?"

"Obviously," the inspector said. He sighed and dabbing his nose with his balled-up tissue. "What do you take me for? That's a basic part of the job."

"I'm sure it is. And what have you found out about them?"

"As a rule, I am not allowed to give you such information."

"Of course, but let me remind you that as a rule, I am not obliged to help you in this sort of investigation. And I suppose that my name has not been mentioned officially in regard to these cases, am I right?"

"I see where you're going with this, Mr. Cooker! You're trying to dig something out of me."

"Which seems appropriate in a cemetery..."

Benjamin could see that Barbaroux was trying to smile. He heard him snicker instead.

"Okay, two can play this idiotic game, but you have to promise absolute discretion. Things are heating up."

"In this investigation, I assure you that things are heating up. The higher-ups are getting agitated, which is affecting the mood in the department. And the reporters are swarming."

"You can at least tell me if there is any connection between the victims?"

"It's unclear at this point. It's possible that they have a connection with the criminal without necessarily having anything to do with one another."

"Do you really believe that?"

"No, not at all. But you have to take everything into consideration. And besides, I wanted to see how you would react to that kind of theory."

Barbaroux sneezed and pinched his nose. Benjamin remained silent, knowing perfectly well that the inspector would eventually part with some information. All he had to do was wait patiently.

In the silence of the cemetery, Benjamin could make out the distant noises: the whiny mopeds, the barking dogs, the construction, the squeals from the schoolyard. They were all signs of life seeping into this final resting place for the dead.

The inspector looked annoyed. He wiped his hand across his face, stomped his feet, and cleared his throat.

"Okay, I'll give you the basic details, and you can sort them out later. Here are the main points. Jules-Ernest Grémillon lived his whole life in that apartment on the Rue Maucoudinat where he was killed. He was actually born there; it belonged to his grandparents and then his parents. He worked for thirty-eight years at the Massip Company. You know it, the old leather company that—"

"Yes, I know Alain Massip very well. He runs the business," Benjamin said. "He has a store on the Places des Grands Hommes and a workshop nearby."

"Grémillon worked at Massip as a leather cutter, and he stayed there until his retirement. Initially, however, he didn't intend to go into this line of work. We found out that he spent almost two years in a seminary. Then, during the war, he didn't seem to have a regular job."

"How did he get by?"

"At that point in time, he seemed to live by his wits. Who knows how? One thing is sure: he was still living with his parents. He seems to have been politically active with two collaborationist groups, Fire and the French Popular Party."

"What was his involvement?"

"It appears that he was a kind of grass-roots organizer. He didn't have anything to do with the leaders of the Vichy government or any other higher-ups. At any rate, I'm not an expert in that area. All I know is that he was some kind of small-time collaborator, fairly unknown. He didn't suffer much at the end of the war. He spent two months in detention. Then he went to work as an oyster grower for a cousin who had a few oyster farms in the Arcachon Basin. In 1949 he found his job as a leather worker in Bordeaux."

"And do you have as much on Émile Chaussagne?" Benjamin asked.

"More or less. He got around more. He came from a middle-class family in Périgueux. He studied the humanities, Latin and Greek, and then went to law school in Bordeaux. When the war broke out, he was still a student, but he dropped everything to concentrate on journalism at some really trashy fascist-leaning newspapers. After the Liberation, it appears that a group of former Resistance fighters wanted him for something or other. They trailed him. According to our intelligence, he lived here and there: Marrakech, Douala, Pondicherry, and Spain, near Alicante. He didn't return to France until 1974, just after Georges Pompidou died, and the old stories were being forgotten. Let's say things worked out for him. He survived on what was left of the family fortune. If I were a novelist, I would say he squandered his inheritance by living parsimoniously. In short, he was starving but was still living like a discreet old gentleman in the Saint Pierre neighborhood."

"And both of them lived just a few blocks apart," Benjamin said. "It would be interesting to know where Armand Jouvenaze lived. He's buried in Libourne, but he might have spent his whole life in Bordeaux. It's strange, all the same—this geographical coincidence, the Saint Pierre neighborhood, and the Pétrus. I can't help but think it's all connected."

"Maybe. Who knows?" Barbaroux said, shrugging.

"You don't seem convinced."

"I think we should focus on their parallel paths during the occupation."

"Indeed, it is rather troubling. You will probably have more clues once you look into the past of this Armand Jouvenaze, who is lying beneath our feet. The Nazi accusation seems especially telling. But why did they break the cross?"

"How the hell should I know?" the inspector growled. He tossed his wadded-up tissue on the grass.

"It was just a simple question, Inspector."

"I'm sorry, Mr. Cooker. But try putting yourself in my shoes! I spent the entire morning dealing with these guys who were rushed over by the prosecutor's office. Almost two hours of ranting and arguing with an old criminologist in a three-piece suit, a long-haired dude in charge of profiling serial killers, and a four-eyed psychiatrist who specializes in dangerousness!"

"Dangerousness. Is that a word?" Benjamin asked, surprised.

"Yes, so it seems. I checked in the dictionary. Another damned word invented by intellectuals who sit at their desks and never go near a corpse. They call Mommy whenever someone gives them the finger. Words: they never run out of them! Those assholes dish them out while they look down at you because they spent ten years at the Sorbonne. And they blurt them out bombastically: 'lack of impulse control,' 'pathogenesis of aggressive behavior,' 'overcompensation of narcissistic weakness,' 'primitive structure of the superego.' I can spit out dozens of phrases like these. Just a bunch of hot air! All I know is this: my men and I, we get stuck with the dirty work—mangled bodies, decomposing cadavers, stench. And we want just one thing: to catch the swine by the balls. So I leave all the theories to the psychobabblers, and they can shove it!"

"There must be something worthwhile in all that. I don't see how those guys can be totally useless."

The inspector took another tissue from his pocket and noisily blew his nose.

"Tell me, Inspector. There's something that intrigues me about you," Benjamin said, smiling.

"What's that?"

"Why do you go to such lengths to appear stupid, when you understand and retain everything people tell you?"

"What I remember most of all is that they send me lazy bums who've spent their careers in the corridors of the prosecutor's office, kissing up to the bigwigs, and treating me like an idiot. 'Barbaroux, he's just a traffic cop! Nothing more than a hillbilly!'"

"You wouldn't happen to have a grudge against Parisians, by any chance?"

"Just a little."

5

Benjamin burst into his office, and his first sight was that of Virgile idly stirring the swirls of cabbage in his soup. The assistant leaped up and flashed a worried smile as the winemaker heaved his frame into a chair. Virgile rushed to the end of the hall to heat more soup in the microwave. He returned with a steaming bowl. Without even a thank-you, Benjamin began to chew his little bits of vegetables with mild disgust.

"You look like you're off your feed, sir."

"You're always there with a clever remark, Virgile."

"No, I just meant that—"

"Your comments are often insightful, but you really hit the nail on the head just now."

Benjamin put his spoon back in the bowl, shoved aside the cabbage, and gulped down more broth. This second day of the diet allowed for no deviation. No fruit to sweeten the regimen, no drink other than unsweetened tea, no corn, peas, or beans. And yet this austere and miraculous soup so lovingly prepared by Elisabeth, with its unbearable odors of old kitchen vegetables, would have seemed delicious had he not been forced to consume it in such great quantities. In order to burn the fat accumulated in a year's worth of rich meals, tastings, and dinners with friends, he knew very well that he had to comply with the discipline. He managed to finish the soup. He put his spoon down with a sigh and frowned at Virgile, who was sitting upright in his chair. He supposed that his assistant was afraid of committing a gaff. In his present mood, he wasn't the most pleasant company.

"Honestly, Virgile, you do not have to join me in this adventure."

"But you don't really need to worry about it."

"Well then, let's just call it a change of routine."

"You could do without it, all the same."

"Wait a minute, what are you talking about, sir?"

"This damned soup, what else?"

"Uh, okay. I thought you wanted to spare me the nasty business of the murders in the Saint Pierre neighborhood."

"Oh no, not at all. You know as well as I do that I never intended to leave you out. I went to the Libourne cemetery after I stopped to see my friend Franck Dubourdieu, and I can assure you that the case is far from resolved."

Benjamin related the latest developments, including the seemingly minor details. He repeated word for word his conversation with Inspector Barbaroux. Benjamin was excited, but he wanted to control his delivery. He likened the process to assessing a military strategy, coming at it from all sides and assiduously evaluating doubts, suppositions, and intuitions.

"As I understand it, sir, we are dealing with someone who is targeting both the living and the dead. There doesn't seem to be anything spontaneous. Everything appears to be premeditated. This serial killer has a certain method, and he's giving us the code."

"We still have to decipher that code."

"Of course, but that is part of his cold reasoning. It appears to be a very calculated and staged revenge."

"Are you implying that part of his scheme is keeping us on his trail?"

"That's what I think. He has something to say, and maybe he reveals a little more each time another victim is found."

"We can't very well wait for him to fill all twelve glasses! Two bodies and one desecration in two days. It's no small matter!"

"Right, he still has nine glasses to fill."

Benjamin opened his cigar box and selected two Villa Zamoranos.

"Dessert, Virgile?"

"Why not?" His assistant smiled and reached for the robusto Benjamin held out to him.

With a clean snip of the guillotine, Benjamin chopped off the vitole and lit it with the brass lighter on his desk blotter. A puff of whitish smoke quickly enveloped them, drawing them further into the puzzle they were trying to solve.

"Evidently all the victims have some kind of connection," Virgile continued. "I'm sure, given their ages and what little is known of their pasts, the connection is related to World War Two."

"It's very likely, Virgile, and that Nazi accusation on the grave marker confirms it. That's not something you do lightly. It must be significant, especially considering what we've learned about Grémillon and Chaussagne since they were murdered."

"I know who might be able to help us," Virgile said, blowing an almost perfect smoke ring toward the ceiling. "It's someone I run into fairly regularly these days."

"Another one of your nightly encounters?" Benjamin joked.

"Not at all, sir. I've been seeing the same girl for some time now. And I've been going out a lot less. She's a homebody. I haven't been to a bar for almost two months, and that's really saying something."

"Be careful, Virgile, domestication is creeping up on you."

"Don't worry, I haven't become that conventional. I just decided to give myself a little break. I've been getting back into sports and swimming laps at the pool. That's where I met the person who could shed some light on this matter. His name is Renaud Duboyne de Ladonnet. He's thirtyish, not the type of guy I would hang out with ordinarily. He's kind of a strange individual, if not downright bizarre. I tried to save him from drowning, but he didn't really need to be saved."

"Hmm, that is odd."

"I was exhausted that day. I had just done fifteen laps, and I was resting at the end of the pool. That's when I saw someone at the bottom. At first I didn't worry, but after about a minute, maybe more, I thought it was fishy. He wasn't moving, and I thought he was in trouble, so I dived down to pull him out. But when I grabbed him to bring him to the surface, he tried to fight me off. It was really a struggle to bring him up. You should have heard how he berated me after I got him out of the water."

"Quite the ingrate," Benjamin said, his cigar wedged in the corner of his mouth.

"In a way. After he calmed down, he explained that he often rested at the bottom of the pool for two minutes to clear his head. It was his way of focusing. Apparently, the lifeguards scold him for it, but he doesn't care."

"And how can he help us?"

"Well, let me tell you. At first I thought he was a nut, but once I started talking to him, I realized he's brilliant. He was very impressed when I told him that I worked for you. He knows some of your books. He's studious and very serious. He has a law degree and speaks fluent English and German. He manages a maritime insurance company and is fascinated by naval history, especially the German World War One military fleet."

Benjamin flicked his ashes into the alabaster ashtray and took another deep puff of his robusto.

"It just so happens that it's World War Two that concerns us," Benjamin said, sending up soft rings of smoke.

"I know, sir. Renaud is an encyclopedia. He owns part of the archives of the former Delmas Company, a maritime insurer that's no longer in business. And he's sitting on a ton of documents dealing with the history of the port of Bordeaux. Also, he's doing research to exonerate his grandfather, a merchant in the Chartrons district who was accused of plundering castles and trafficking in art on behalf of Hermann Goering. Renaud wants to clear his name."

"I say, your friend seems very busy," Benjamin said, straightening up in his chair. "And where does he get this passion for German history?"

"I don't know, exactly. Although he's a pacifist himself, his father was an officer in Indochina and Algeria, and that's why he's interested in anything having to do with the military. His passion for Germany stems from an affair he had with a student from Bavaria. His 'valkyrie,' as he calls her, went back to Munich, and they still talk on the phone at least once a week. I don't ask him about her—you know I don't like to pry—but I think it explains why he doesn't look at any of the girls at the pool. And I can tell you there are some real knockouts, if I do say so myself."

"What's the family name, again?"

"Duboyne de Ladonnet, with two *n*'s, not like *canelé*. That's what I said to myself when he spelled it for me. You've noticed how people often write *canelé* with two *n*'s?"

Benjamin ignored this mnemonic observation about Bordeaux's well-known pastries and used his armrests to push himself out of his chair. Once on his feet, he waved away the cloud of smoke that was keeping him from seeing where he wanted to go. Then he began pacing the room. He needed to stretch his legs.

"Renaud Duboyne de Ladonnet," he murmured. "That does not ring a bell."

"If you'd like, I could introduce you to him. He lives on the Cours de Verdun, not far from the public gardens."

"Why not? What do we have to lose?"

§ § §

The meeting was arranged for just before noon the following day at a secondhand bookstore in the Saint Pierre neighborhood. It was in an old warehouse that had once housed exotic merchandise and dreams of grandeur. After spending the morning on the Languedoc-Roussillon tastings, Benjamin and Virgile had carefully filed away their notes in a laboratory cabinet and arrived a quarter of an hour early. They immediately took advantage of the opportunity to rummage through the store's dusty shelves and immerse themselves in old books on the history of Bordeaux.

All was quiet in the shop until the bell at the door plinked. Benjamin turned and saw a man with thick glasses distorting his eyes and a tight raincoat buttoned up to his chin. Renaud Duboyne de Ladonnet walked down the center aisle and came to greet Benjamin and Virgile with firm handshakes. His trousers, which barely covered his ankles, revealed a pair of black loafers in need of polish, yet his perfect manners and sharp-mindedness came through.

"Thank you for making yourself available on such short notice," said Benjamin.

"Not at all. It's the least I could do for someone who tried to save my life," Renaud answered dryly.

"Virgile told me how you met. And I don't need to tell you that Virgile is a virtual lifesaver. Without him, I don't know how we could get all our work done at Cooker & Co."

Virgile remained quiet and gave an earnest smile that looked just a tad self-deprecating. Benjamin didn't mention one of the characteristics he liked most about his assistant: that he was confident, but never cocky.

"According to Virgile," the winemaker continued, "you are fascinated with German military history, and you also seem to be intimately familiar with our city's history."

"What exactly do you want to know?"

"Almost everything about life in Bordeaux during the occupation."

"That's quite a topic. The more I study the history of this city, the more I realize it's a bottomless well."

"I understand. I have the same feeling about wine. The further I go, the less I know."

"I am not surprised, and I believe this insight speaks well of you. I've read some of your books, most recently last season's *Cooker Guide*, and I must say I was touched by your modesty and your care to never judge prematurely. This humility comes through, even when you take a position."

"Perhaps you can at least give me a small overview of that era so that I can grasp the essential points? I've always felt the need to immerse myself in history and geography and visualize the countryside, the scenery, the clothing, and faces. They help me form my thoughts and establish my opinions."

"That's the kind of sensitivity I appreciate in a historian. In a nutshell, I can tell you that Bordeaux and the entire Aquitaine region experienced pretty much what the rest of France experienced: the same indifference and the same magnanimity, spinelessness and bravery, cowardice and heroism, selfishness and generosity. You find a bit of everything."

"So, the worst and the best, you say. You can talk to me frankly. I have no illusions about human beings, even though I have faith in humanity."

"I see. Well then, knowing the history of Bordeaux during the occupation will either strengthen your belief in humanity or feed your doubts."

"What do you know about political movements like the French Popular Party and the group called Fire?" Benjamin asked casually.

Renaud Duboyne de Ladonnet seemed to hesitate. He pushed his glasses up his nose, folded his arms, and pursed his lips before answering.

"From the start of the occupation, collaborationist groups sprang up all over the country, and some of them took root in this area. One of them was the French Popular Party, led by Jacques Doriot, a communist who was converted to fascism. Another was the National Popular Rally, founded by Marcel Déat. They were two large political groups under Marshal Pétain. I won't go into the various theories that were expounded in all the propaganda they disseminated."

"Was there a lot of support for these people in Bordeaux?"

"Yes, there was. It's rather shocking, in fact. In any case, even the Vichy sympathizers who weren't card-carrying members of any party cheered on their little leaders. More than three thousand people were at the Athenaeum to welcome Déat on May 17, 1941. He was invited by his friend Adrien Marquet, the mayor of Bordeaux and minister of the interior in the Vichy government. People were clamoring to get in to hear him talk. The topic was the New France in the New Europe. And there were dozens of meetings and rallies of this ilk all over Bordeaux. You can't imagine how many talks were organized on anti-Semitism, national reconstruction, the evils of freemasonry, Bolshevism, capitalism, the glory of Germanic myths, and the war on stateless people. And, of course, there were the countless leaflets and posters."

"In addition to these two main organizations, I imagine there were other groups," Benjamin interjected. "What do you know about the group called Fire?"

The bookstore owner, who had been unpacking and organizing old paperbacks at the back of the store, walked over to the cash register and sat down. Renaud Duboyne de Ladonnet waited until he was settled and took two steps to the side. Benjamin listened carefully as he enumerated the various movements and factions that proliferated more or less successfully during the war.

The Fire group was really no more than an ephemeral spark. It never claimed more than three dozen members, Renaud told Benjamin. The group was led by a fanatic destined for mediocrity, a certain Maurice Delauney. He had started the newspaper *La Tempête* in 1941 to spread his hatred of Jews and everyone else he deemed responsible for France's degradation. Before this puppet group disappeared, it was headquartered at 22 Cours Clemenceau.

"A multitude of groups emerged, and some French citizens embraced them with queasy fervor," Renaud said. "The organizations advocated collaboration with Nazi Germany and a purging of liberal demons and Judeo-Masonic riffraff. Each one of these organizations had committees in the provinces, and Bordeaux was a strategic platform for spreading the doctrine in the region. Among them were the Social Revolutionary Movement, built on the ruins of the Cagoule and led by Eugène Deloncle, headquartered at 1 Rue du Maréchal-Joffre; Francisme, founded by Marcel Bucard, a fascist organization in line with Mussolini's precepts that eventually petered out; the French League, whose members blindly followed Pierre Costantini and whose most active subsidiary in the Gironde was established in Arcachon in June 1942; the facist Falange at 16 Rue Barada, directed by Pierre Paparan, who owed allegiance to SS leader Herbert Hagen; the French National-Collectivist Party and its branch at 50 Cours Clemenceau; and the Socialist French National Front at 27 Rue Gouvion, with forty followers united under the Pétain flag."

Renaud's historical knowledge seemed endless. He was eager to share information and made no attempt to conceal the muddy twists and turns France had gotten caught up in. In a low voice he recalled how fear dominated the region in those days. Civilian and paramilitary organizations did their insidious work in the dark. Those groups also included the Anti-Bolshevik Action Committee, the Legion of French Volunteers, the Legionary Order Service, the Corps of French Volunteers, and Milice, whose regional offices were at 11 Cours Tournon. That organization was under the leadership of Vichy Lieutenant Colonel Robert Franc.

Renaud took a breath and exhaled, as if trying to expel the black plague of that time period in French history.

"Do the names Jules-Ernest Grémillon, Émile Chaussagne, and Armand Jouvenaze ring a bell, by any chance?" Benjamin asked.

"You know, Mr. Cooker, chance rarely plays a part in this type of research. It just takes work, lots of it, and patience, and a bit of self-sacrifice. Searching the archives again and again, consulting official documents, and then, of course, studying the papers that are much less well-known, if not secret..."

"What kind?"

"I cannot tell you or even reveal my methods, but please understand that conventional routes do not always pay off, and sometimes you have to know the shortcuts."

"Could you possibly help me flush out some information on these three names?"

"Out of context, nothing comes to mind."

"Would you like me to write them down on a piece of paper?"

"No need for that. I have them in my head. I'm able to retain all sorts of details. It's a must in my line of work. The slightest clue, the faintest allusion, the smallest piece of information can lead to a breakthrough. I'll see what I can do, but don't be too optimistic. It could take a long time, and it might end in disappointment."

"Take all the time you need," Benjamin said. He looked Renaud in the eye through the distorted lenses of his glasses. "I think we'll be seeing each other again."

6

Against all odds, Benjamin Cooker was entering the third day of his diet with newfound serenity. The evening before, Elisabeth had greeted him in Grangebelle's kitchen with a baked potato, a priceless reward of succulent warmth, which he savored to the last bite. On this day he would be allowed fresh fruits and green vegetables, in addition to his cabbage soup. Resisting the seductive window displays of *foie gras* and truffles at Dubernet and *canelés* at Baillardran, Benjamin headed on foot toward the Grands Hommes shopping center.

He walked under the glass dome of the shopping center, which spilled light over the vast array of merchandise. After stopping at the newsstand to pick up his papers and magazines on winemaking and tableware, he took the circular aisle that led to the leather shop. A man in his sixties with dazzling white hair that was closely cropped and a round bearded face greeted him from behind the window. Benjamin waved to him, indicating he did not want to bother him in his shop but preferred to wait outside.

Alain Massip was a classy gentleman whom Benjamin regretted not seeing more often. They had many things in common. They both tended to be dandies, albeit refined dandies. They valued well-made conservative clothing and had a taste for beautiful objects, fine food, and elegant convertibles. Each was brilliant, but also reserved. They also shared an amused detachment regarding money, a caustic regard for the antics of powerful people, a desire for spirituality and social justice, and an irrepressible zest for life despite the grief that often derailed it.

Massap, however, was more extroverted than Benjamin. The winemaker unconsciously took a step back when the leather merchant patted him warmly on the shoulder while shaking his hand.

"What a surprise, Benjamin! How are you?"

"Hello, Alain, I can't pretend that I was just walking by. I need a favor, or rather, some information."

"In that case, we'll be more comfortable in the workshop. Follow me!"

They left the shopping center and crossed the street to a building whose façade had been recently renovated. They went up to the second floor of the building's annex, where the strong odor of leather, mixed with the sweet fragrance of glue, permeated the air. Two employees were bent over large worktables, where they measured, cut, and sewed swatches of finely cured kidskin. Alain made his way to a workbench cluttered with silver buckles and showed Benjamin a handbag. It was made of soft pink leather and featured a locking mechanism and adjustable strap that were particularly clever. Alain told Benjamin that this was a prototype. He planned to introduce a line of handbags in a range of colors the following season.

Alain Massip's energy and piercing eyes expressed his passion for the mysteries of this craft, which he had worked hard to preserve for many years. His enthusiasm was contagious, and Benjamin listened attentively, thinking how much this man had to love women. He was able to fulfill their desires, anticipate their needs and whims, pay attention to their complaints, and attend to their concerns, all with the aim of making their lives more convenient and pleasurable.

"I could listen to you for hours, Alain. But unfortunately, I am short on time," the winemaker said, picking up a scrap of granulated leather and rubbing it between his fingers. "I need you to give me some information on Jules-Ernest Grémillon."

"I read about his murder in the *Sud-Ouest*," Massip said. The smile disappeared from his face. "It's really horrendous! And to think that things like that happen so close to us!"

Benjamin knew that nothing about the ritual of the twelve glasses had been reported on television or in the newspapers and that no information had been leaked by the police department. He trusted his friend's discretion but decided to say nothing. He didn't want to betray Inspector Barbaroux's trust.

"Please don't ask me why I want to know certain things about this man. It's a rather sensitive situation, but I found out that he worked here for a long time."

"Yes, indeed, my father hired him in the early nineteen fifties. He spent nearly forty years with the company. He was primarily a cutter, and he was an excellent employee, according to what my father told me. It's hard to find really good workers these days."

"I'm sure that's true."

"I wasn't with the company when he started, but it seems he learned the trade quickly, and he knew how to do just about everything. We never had any complaints about him."

"Did you know him well?"

"Well, I worked alongside him when I was just learning the trade, before I became a manager. But I didn't really know him. He was reserved, quiet, very soft-spoken."

"Do you know anything about his political leanings or his past in Bordeaux?"

"Not in the least. He was the silent type."

"It seems he had some big problems after the liberation because of his connections with the collaborationists. You never heard him talk about that?"

"If my father had known, he would have fired him on the spot. You know very well that's not the kind of company we run."

"You never even caught wind of it, even as a rumor?"

"I'm telling you that he would not have been allowed to remain here if we had known. My father was interned in Germany. He was a prisoner of war in the Vosges and sent to a brick factory in Kandern, where he finally escaped with two buddies. As a matter of fact, he left a written account for us and our descendants."

Alain went over to a shelf and picked up a document covered in a reddish brown dust jacket. In twenty single-spaced typed pages, Maurice Massip had recorded his experiences in an internment camp so that future generations would know. Despite the fear, cold, harsh working conditions, and privations, he had found the strength to break out and reach the Swiss border. Benjamin skimmed the text, written with precision but without grandiloquence or moral preaching. It retraced the ordeal and described the escape. His hope came through in each sentence:

The forest was close by. We made it to the trees. But we couldn't stop. We had to keep going, farther and farther. And we did. Our hearts were beating hard in our chests. We were terrified that we would hear the men shouting and the dogs barking at any moment. We forged on, out of breath and our legs so weak, they almost refused to carry us. Still we moved forward, toward freedom.

"It's a priceless record," Benjamin murmured. The man's bravery in the face of such fear and darkness had moved him.

"I brought it here to the workshop to restore it a little and reinforce the binding. But the main thing is, I handed it over to my children so that they would know who their grandfather was, and eventually they can have their children read it. It's important."

"Excuse me for insisting, but getting back to Grémillon, can you at least tell me what sort of life he led?"

"Work was really the only place we saw him. I can tell you that he never married. And I don't believe he had any serious relationships. At least none that I know of. I think his primary pleasure was an occasional game of pool with friends."

"French billiards, I presume?"

"Exactly. I was much younger then, but as I recall, they would go to the same place, a seedy café called Chez Joseph in the Mériadeck quarter before it was razed and replaced with depressing concrete they call urban renewal."

"Do you remember his friends?"

"Guys his age. They looked more or less the same. They weren't very chatty either."

"Do you have any of their names?"

"It was all so long ago."

"Not a single detail?"

"I think one of them was called Armand. Yes, that's it, Armand."

"Armand. Was that his first or his last name?"

"First, I think. But I'm not sure. He'd come by sometimes to pick up Jules-Ernest in a Dauphine sports car, a red one. That I'm sure of!"

"Is that all?"

"Yes, sorry."

"Well, I'll make do with that. Thanks all the same!"

Benjamin shook hands with Alain Massip and promised to stop by before the end of the month to have lunch at Noailles. He went down the stairs, nearly slipping on the bottom step, and found himself in the street under a fine rain.

"Hey, Benjamin, don't run off!"

The winemaker turned and looked up. Alain was leaning from a window on the second floor of the building. "Sometimes there was another guy in the Dauphine," Alain shouted, his hands cupped around his mouth. "I think they called him 'the Bull.' But he wasn't really a brute."

"What do you mean?" Benjamin strained to hear Alain above the traffic noise.

"He was more of a weakling, this Bull. It must have been a nickname from darts, you know, because of hitting the bull's-eye."

§ § §

Coming through the door to the Cooker & Co. offices on the Allées de Tourny, Benjamin was pleased to find Franck Dubourdieu sipping bergamot tea with his secretary, Jacqueline. Obviously charmed by her boss's distinguished colleague, Jacqueline was nodding and playing with her gold bracelet, which dripped gaudy and jangly trinkets. Benjamin poured himself a cup of tea and invited Dubourdieu to follow him.

"Ever since you came by my house, I've been thinking about this business," Dubourdieu said as soon as they were in Benjamin's office. "I think I have some information that might help you."

"I was sure you would look into the matter. To tell the truth, I would have been surprised if you hadn't."

"You are wicked, Benjamin. You knew that if you threw a bottle into the sea, I would jump in to see what was in it."

"Especially if it was a bottle of Pétrus!"

"Precisely. I tasted the samples you had Inspector Barbaroux send over. It's rather astonishing. I went back several times, and I let some time elapse between each tasting. I still have the same impression."

"You're confirming what you said before about the vintage?"

"But my opinion is more nuanced now. I found some characteristics of a great wine, but they were mostly in the aroma. The body did not match up. The more I think about it, the more I am leaning toward a 1942."

"You don't say," Benjamin said, surprised at his friend's certainty. "That's not your usual style, to be so sure."

"I did take care to verify my opinion before coming here to meet you. I managed to obtain two bottles so that I could be as certain as possible."

"Don't tell me you went out of your way to unearth bottles dating from World War Two. I can't believe it. You wouldn't care to reveal your source, would you?"

"Don't ask me. I promised to be very hush–hush about it."

Benjamin understood he had just been one-upped. He attempted to keep his pride intact. "I think I know where they come from, anyway."

"That's not very likely. At any rate, you won't find out from me. Besides, it doesn't matter how I got them. The main thing is moving forward with the investigation, isn't it?"

"That's true enough."

"That said, my evaluation isn't one hundred percent guaranteed, especially because there is a slight difference between the samples."

"Exactly. It's almost imperceptible, but I'm delighted to hear you confirm it, because I wasn't really sure."

"If you continue along that line of reasoning, it seems obvious that the killer is using several bottles. The vintage is the same for all of them, but some have been affected by aging."

The theory seemed viable, and they were silent while the bronze clock atop the tall file cabinet ticked away the minutes. Benjamin was weighing the information, cross-referencing his deductions, and correcting any biased speculation to satisfy his need for a rational explanation. He knew his friend, also absorbed in thought, was doing the same thing, and he reflected on something the French politician Pierre-Joseph Proudhon had written: "As long as man knows little, he inevitably talks much. The less he reasons, the more he babbles."

"So it's someone who has several old bottles of Pétrus," Benjamin said, fiddling with the worn edge of his leather desk blotter. "Someone who has the means to leave priceless bottles as his calling card."

"And who couldn't care less about wasting them that way!" said Dubourdieu. "It's also possible that this person doesn't know what they are worth."

"I don't agree with you there. I think it's more likely that the person knows their value, and that gives his murders even more meaning. His calling card is rare. In fact unique!"

"I have my doubts," Dubourdieu said. "But whether this person knows the value of the wine or not, it may well have some significance above and beyond what it's worth."

"Are you sure you can't tell me where you got your bottles?" Benjamin hated having to ask again, but he disliked being kept in the dark even more.

"I can only tell you that it was a very special moment, and that the bottles were well preserved."

"I hope you didn't have to pay for them."

"Don't worry. I didn't do anything foolish."

"It's true that no one, or almost no one, can afford them," Benjamin said wearily. "For the old vintages that can still be found, the prices I've seen online are staggering. As for the last sales at auction, it's not even worth talking about."

"Remember that bottle from 1947 that was auctioned off at more than twenty-two hundred euros in February of 1999? And that was a steal at the time."

"Of course. It was in mint condition. The label was impeccable, and the bottle hadn't been moved much at all. A bottle like that would be worth much more now!"

"Maybe I can't afford every bottle I come across, but I'll keep doing this work until I'm on my deathbed," Dubourdieu joked. "Having access to great wines is a pleasure and privilege."

The two men began a meticulous inventory of their respective tastings. Apart from two or three points, they agreed on the basics. Benjamin reveled in exploring this territory with his friend. Both were privy to well-guarded secrets that often made their work look like esoteric magic to an outsider.

Benjamin and Dubourdieu were fortunate to have archival memories, which served them well in their interests and fields of expertise. Dubourdieu, could list complete discographies of bebop and West Coast jazz, including dates of shows, titles of every recorded session piece, the names of contributing musicians, and sometimes even their unreleased recordings. He could also tick off all the producers and sound engineers. Benjamin, for his part, could reel off hundreds of quotes by major and minor writers. He favored Oscar Wilde and Winston Churchill, whom his father, Paul William, claimed as a distant relative.

Dubourdieu enumerated all the spectacular years for Pétrus. Starting in 1947 and ending in 2000, there were ten of them. "Those were huge years: 1947, 1959, 1961, 1964, 1970, 1982, 1995, 1996, 1998, and 2000!" Dubourdieu said, his face animated.

"They were miraculous years!" Benjamin, carried away by his enthusiasm, was almost shouting. He agreed with his friend that there were no mediocre Pétruses, only a few that weren't quite as successful. Some needed to be consumed sooner than others, and these were not the jewels of the domain. But even a harshly judged Pétrus was better than most other great wines. The demands of the harvest, the special attention to the farming methods, the winemaking process elevated to a fine art—nothing was left to chance by this producer, which jealously guarded its mysteries and prestige.

Benjamin and Dubourdieu agreed that the 1978 was one of the rare disappointing Pétruses. All merlots had suffered greatly that year, but those in following vintages had kept their promise. Several wines from the nineteen eighties had been remarkable, and the 1995 and the 1998 surpassed all expectations. Some flowed in the glass like a dream, whether austere or smooth, tannic or silky, intense or light, exuberant or reserved. In each case, the Pétrus was an elegant wine, full-bodied, always distinguished, luminous, ample, and harmonious in the mouth. It had varying aromas of black and purple fruits, wood, licorice, cinnamon, raspberry, and truffle.

When Virgile Lanssien burst into his office, Benjamin was expressing his regret at not having had the chance to taste the 1950, 1952, 1953, and 1954, at their peak, toward the end of the nineteen sixties.

"Sorry to disturb you, sir. Inspector Barbaroux would like to meet with you. He is waiting at 75 Rue des Bahutiers!"

"Right now?"

"So I believe."

§ § §

Benjamin was in a (fowl) mood when he arrived with his assistant at the crime-scene tape blocking the way to the Saint Pierre neighborhood. He had said good-bye to his friend Franck Dubourdieu a little too brusquely but promised to invite him to dinner at Grangebelle. He would have a bottle of Pétrus on hand. That was the least he could do and a lovely way to ask forgiveness for breaking off their nearly rapturous visit. Perhaps Elisabeth would prepare the leg of venison in their freezer.

They would savor it with a thick *grand veneur* red wine sauce. Just thinking about it made him salivate and eagerly anticipate the day he could finally banish the lingering odor of cabbage soup.

In the apartment, the inspector greeted them with a sly grin. Benjamin didn't think it was quite appropriate. He spotted two bare legs on the green linoleum but couldn't see the rest of the body, as it was behind a brown velour armchair. The winemaker made the sign of the cross without attempting to camouflage his gesture. Behind the armchair, two officers from the forensics team were bending over the body. Benjamin, scanning the wrinkled skin and purple varicose veins on the legs, guessed that the victim was elderly.

"Édouard Prébourg, eighty-eight years old. Same demise."

"And the glasses again?" Benjamin asked, still staring at the legs.

"Four wine glasses filled and eight empty, as you would expect. The same staging!"

Benjamin told Virgile to wait in the hallway while he tasted the wine in the living room. The woman in the white coat, who had been at all the previous scenes, asked the captain for permission to cover the body with a blanket. It was a sight the winemaker didn't need to see, she said.

"You don't think he's afraid of an old pair of balls, do you?" the inspector responded.

Barbaroux let out a hearty laugh. Benjamin saw the woman shudder. He pretended that he hadn't heard the exchange and proceeded with the tasting. He brought each glass to his lips, turned toward the inspector, and shrugged.

"Send the samples to the same person," he said simply. "You know who it is. I've just come from my office, where I was talking with him."

"That's all you have to say?" Barbaroux asked. He wasn't grinning now. He looked concerned.

"I'm expected at my lab, and I don't have time to stay," Benjamin grumbled as he mopped his forehead with a handkerchief.

"But I have a number of things to ask you."

"If you don't mind, we'll see to all that tomorrow."

The winemaker didn't give the inspector a chance to pursue the conversation. He turned on his heels, nodded good-bye to the forensics team, and walked out of the living room, taking care to look away from the bloody remains of Édouard Prébourg.

The afternoon was long and tedious. Alexandrine de la Palussière had methodically prepared the testing. And Benjamin, assisted by the careful and silent Virgile, tasted no fewer than sixty-three wines from Languedoc-Roussillon without uttering a word. He tasted, spat into the sink, made notes, and repeated the process over and over with a determination verging on obsession. Beads of sweat formed at his temples, and now and then he wiped them away while gritting his teeth. Benjamin knew he was swearing far too much. He hardly ever swore, and now he had done it five times in the space of a few hours. Virgile was surely becoming concerned. He knew his assistant had never seen him so much on edge.

At the end of the day, Benjamin felt nauseous and dizzy. He almost fainted. Virgile ran over to keep Benjamin from falling and grabbed a chair for him. As usual, Virgile's gestures were clumsy. He didn't seem to know exactly how to help. Benjamin grumbled and asked to be left in peace. He dismissed his assistant with the wave of a hand and an irritated sigh. He waited for the nausea to subside, stood up slowly, and left without saying good-bye to the rest of the staff.

Once on the street, Benjamin breathed in the cold night air and walked carefully toward the Allées de Tourny. At his side, Virgile looked anxious and frightened.

"We're going to the office?"

"So it appears," Benjamin grumbled.

"Maybe it's not a good idea to go back to work so late, especially after that fainting spell you just had."

"Who says I'm going to work? I'm going to the office to get warm and heat up the rest of that soup before I drive home!"

Once in the hallway, Benjamin threw his coat over a chair and headed toward the microwave. He didn't even bother to turn on the lights. There was enough illumination from the streetlights outside to see where he was going.

"Please, let me warm up the soup for you," Virgile said as he turned on the overhead lights.

"Let me do it, for heaven's sake. I didn't ask you!"

"It's all ready to go. Just set the timer for a minute and a half," the assistant dared to say as he slipped behind Jacqueline's empty desk.

Benjamin struggled with the microwave and cursed the "fucking electronic piece of shit" twice before punching in the numbers and slamming the door shut. He didn't hear Virgile pick up Jacqueline's phone. Nor did he hear his assistant talking in hushed tones with Elisabeth, who had been waiting for him at Grangebelle.

"Mrs. Cooker? I hope I am not disturbing you."

"Not at all, my dear Virgile."

"You really have to do something for your husband, ma'am."

"But what can I do for you? Speak up, I can hardly hear you."

"I'm worried about him," the assistant whispered. "He just had a dizzy spell…"

"Nothing serious, I hope?"

"No, rest assured. But in my opinion, he's dying of hunger. He can't take it anymore!"

"Probably a little hypoglycemia. He needs to eat his soup regularly throughout the day."

"You know him. He doesn't always have the time."

"I'm counting on your influence, Virgile," Elisabeth said.

"There's more to it, Mrs. Cooker. He's really not easy... How can I say it? Well, he's almost impossible to bear since you put him on that diet. Please forgive me for being so blunt."

"I've been thinking of you these last few days, and I do feel sorry for you, Virgile. I can only imagine the foul mood he's been in at the office."

"Well, actually, as a matter of fact, 'foul' is exactly the word for it. I would never want to interfere in your personal life, ma'am, but I do hope you understand what I'm getting at. Are you sure that we have to do this diet thing all the way to day seven?"

7

The two representatives of Cooker & Co. were greeted with deference by a sallow-complexioned maid with gray hair. She invited them into the living room to await Renaud Duboyne de Ladonnet. She offered them tea, which they happily accepted as they sat down awkwardly on the worn cushions of the Louis XV chairs. The apartment was posh without being the least bit flashy. Everything around them suggested the faded comfort and timeless elegance of provincial aristocracy. The woodwork, crown molding, and stucco rosettes on the ceiling, the printed fabric on the walls, the thick velour curtains held in place by silk braided tiebacks: the entire décor seemed to have weathered the decades without succumbing to the influence of fashion.

The master of the house arrived. He was out of breath, and his face was pink and sweaty. He greeted them with firm handshakes and sat down in the closest chair without bothering to remove his raincoat, buttoned to the chin, as usual. Renaud Duboyne de Ladonnet blended perfectly with his apartment: his stiff and formal demeanor, his dated hairstyle, the thick lenses of his glasses, which curiously matched the thick crystals hanging from the chandeliers, his signet ring, which mirrored the cherrywood coat of arms on the fireplace, the cut of his trench coat, the rumpled corduroy pants hemmed too high, the patina of his shoes on the worn threads of the Persian carpet. Everything about him seemed in perfect harmony with this antiquated theater, which was custom-made for an obsessive and nostalgic historian.

Benjamin had recovered his strength and forgotten his scare of the night before. This fourth day of the diet promised to be more flexible. To the inevitable cabbage soup, three bananas and a quart of skimmed milk had been added. His efforts were further rewarded when he stepped on the scale as he came out of the shower and found that he had lost seven pounds. His wife had kissed him on the chest and pinched his hips. She had then become quite affectionate in the warm steam of the bathroom. Still enveloped in Elisabeth's gardenia perfume, he had left Grangebelle three-quarters of an hour late but with a light heart and a soothed mind.

Renaud, still in his raincoat, asked his housekeeper to prepare another pot of tea. He got out of his chair, walked over to a small card table, and picked up a black dossier cinched with a beige ribbon. He returned to his chair and slowly opened the document.

"I've done some research for you, gentlemen, and I've finally found a bit of information on Jules-Ernest Grémillon. He belonged to the Fire group, starting in January, 1941. A few months later he joined the National Popular Rally. He also belonged to the Association of Friends of Marshall Pétain, which had a rather active committee in the region."

"What do you mean by active?" Benjamin asked, resting his cup on the rosewood-inlay table beside his chair.

"They organized many high-profile undertakings and much propaganda, meetings and shows, theatrical performances, and sporting events, as well as some charitable activities, especially regular visits to needy families. Members also worked in the Médoc vineyards, as did some members of the Malice française."

"Well, what do you know!" Virgile exclaimed, his eyes wide. The Milice française was a much-feared paramilitary organization during the occupation, well known for the tactics it used against the Resistance. "I had no idea that members of this militia also worked in the vineyards to compensate for the lack of manpower."

"Absolutely!" Renaud said. "I don't have the exact list of all the estates that accepted their help, but there were quite a few. It would have been senseless to refuse such valuable help when most men were away from home."

"And was this only in the Médoc?" Benjamin asked. "Never in the Pomerol area, by any chance?"

"How do I know? Perhaps, but I have no information about that."

Benjamin sensed that Renaud was embarrassed. He didn't seem to like admitting that he lacked an important piece of information. The young man strove to be infallible and no doubt would correct this gap in his self-education.

"The wine world was especially disrupted by the war," Renaud went on, picking up a batch of hastily scribbled sheets of paper. "Especially since certain Nazi dignitaries were quite fond of grand cru wines. Hermann Goering was crazy about Bordeaux wines, while Joseph Goebbels preferred Burgundies. Incidentally, they quickly set up a whole system allowing them to amass a fortune in French wines. Several so-called *weinführers* were assigned to the biggest French wine-growing regions at the beginning of the occupation. They were in charge of acquiring the best wines and having them transported to Germany. Of course, it was expected that they would pay the lowest price possible and resell at huge profits in the international market. In Bordeaux, there was a man named Heinz Bömers who was at the mercy of Goering's whims. He seemed to be a decent man, rather... How can I describe him?"

Renaud hesitated and pushed his thick glasses back up his nose as he searched for just the right words to describe this German, whose reputation he obviously did not want to sully. Their host's silence dragged on a bit, and Virgile poured himself another cup of tea. Benjamin finally decided to get them back on track.

"I haven't discussed this painful period with many people from Bordeaux, but some old landowners have spoken about him in mostly positive terms."

"I'm not surprised that you've heard about him," Renaud said. "The Bömers, who were an upper-class family from Bremen, were very involved in wine brokering before the war. And when Heinz, who inherited the business, was forced to accept the job of agent for the Nazis—or put his family at risk—he managed to do so on his own terms. He refused to wear the Nazi uniform, to plunder châteaux, or to allow any abuses by the troops. Strangely enough, Hermann Goering, who hated the Bömers family, was the one who sent him to Bordeaux."

"Was it the Bömers who owned the Château Smith-Haut-Lafitte before World War One?" Benjamin asked.

"Exactly! Because they were German expats, their property was expropriated during the First

World War. But after the war, they were still able
to maintain close ties in the region. That's why this
weinführer was welcomed by everyone in the business when he arrived after the Franco-German
armistice was signed in 1940. Even though he was
working for the Germans, Heinz Bömers was a
decent guy and a Francophile at heart. He was
accommodating and had kept up relations with
certain companies in Bordeaux. All the wine
producers adapted to the situation, and there was
no other choice but to sell to Germany, because
the American and British markets were closed.
Otherwise, what would they have done with all
their wine? Dump it into the Garonne River?"

"How much wine are we talking about, more
or less?"

"It varied. He could easily buy almost a million bottles in one order. Suffice it to say that the
Chartrons merchants were eager to please when
the *weinführer* took an interest in their companies.
For his part, he hated people who thought they
needed to grovel at his feet. He behaved rather
well. His prices were appropriate for the most part,
and I think it's fair to say he helped the Bordeaux
region sell off the medium-quality wine that
congested the warehouses after the bad vintages
of the nineteen thirties. By the way, his attitude
was not necessarily looked upon favorably by the
higher-ups. Goering summoned him to Berlin
three times to reprimand him."

The teapot was empty and Renaud called his housekeeper, who appeared so quickly, Benjamin thought she might have been listening at the door. She picked up the teapot and left without acknowledging Benjamin or Virgile. Her colorless complexion and white hair blended in with the room's washed-out colors.

"I imagine you've heard of Louis Eschenauer?" the host asked, slipping a piece of onionskin paper out of the dossier.

"The one everyone in Chartrons called Uncle Louis?" Benjamin said. "He was a strange fellow, it seems."

"To say the least," Renaud agreed, exposing his teeth in a foolish-looking grin. "He was seventy years old during the occupation, and you could say he had already seen a thing or two."

"Never heard of him!" Virgile interjected.

"You might not have, but you're certainly familiar with the Eschenauer family. They were from Alsace originally, but they have been important wine merchants and estate owners in Bordeaux since 1821. This particular Eschenauer was an amiable man—he was also called the king of Bordeaux—and very clever, as well. During Prohibition in the United States, for example, he pulled off a fabulous scheme to send Sauternes and other white wines to American clients in crystal vials labeled 'Roman bath water.' He did very well with that. More tea, gentlemen?"

Benjamin and Virgile held out their cups and made themselves comfortable in their chairs to listen to the adventures of this character nicknamed Uncle Louis. With statistics in hand, Renaud described his business activities and risky investments, his passion for modern art, his stable of race horses, his numerous sports cars, his romantic disappointments, his eccentricities, his winter vacations in Egypt, and his friendship with Joachim von Ribbentrop, who, once he had become foreign affairs minister of the Third Reich, had helped him increase his revenues considerably.

"When the war broke out, more than half of his company's business was already coming from Germany, and it seemed natural to continue this relationship when Bömers, the *weinführer*, arrived in Bordeaux, especially because Louis Eschenauer was the uncle of Captain Ernst Kühnemann, the German wine merchant who had been given command of Bordeaux's port," Renaud explained.

"Virgile, here's an intriguing tidbit: at the time Uncle Louis owned Le Chapon Fin, where we've enjoyed many a fine meal. Uncle Louis used the restaurant to entertain Kühnemann, Bömers, and other prominent Germans. Needless to say, the German patrons of Le Chapon Fin were not subject to any restrictions and obviously enjoyed the best crus of Médoc, Saint-Émilion, and beyond."

Renaud shifted in his seat and went on, "Uncle Louis was a show-off, arrogant, and smug about his successes to the point of arousing resentment among his acquaintances in Bordeaux. And he was as opportunistic as they come. For example, he snatched up two Jewish estates after they had been abandoned. He kept them productive during the occupation. But no one ever heard him utter a disparaging remark about the Jews. Many of the Rothschilds had fled Bordeaux, and Baron Philippe de Rothschild had joined the British military. It's believed that Uncle Louis interceded for the Rothschilds while they were gone and succeeded in keeping much of the estate's wine from being seized. It's also believed that he did much behind the scenes to protect the city of Bordeaux, as well as the region. After the allied invasion, his nephew was given the assignment of destroying the port. Although this hasn't been confirmed, some think the port was spared because of Uncle Louis."

Benjamin and Virgile sipped at their tea without a word.

"When the Resistance forces arrested him a few days after the occupying forces left, he really did not realize the danger he was in. He defended himself poorly and was sentenced to two years in prison. His property was seized, and he was forced to pay a penalty of sixty-two million francs. In addition, he was permanently banned from doing business in Bordeaux," Renaud continued.

"In my opinion, Uncle Louis was made an example because he had a high profile during the occupation," Renaud said as he blew on his steaming tea. "But he certainly wasn't the only businessman who collaborated with the enemy, and as far as I'm concerned, he had no blood on his hands. I don't even think he bought into the Nazi ideology. Compared with certain crooks who made out just fine, they were unduly harsh with Uncle Louis. Just compare his case with Maurice Papon's."

"That scum!" Virgile said, gritting his teeth.

"I wouldn't say that, exactly," Benjamin said calmly. "Papon was worse than scum. He was a behind-the-scenes criminal with no conscience. The worst possible kind. I've always wondered how a fairly intelligent and well-educated guy could agree to send hundreds of people to their death. As simple that, with a stroke of his pen! Just a signature at the bottom of a business form!"

Virgile nodded while Renaud leafed through the file.

"Accomplice to murder, abuse of authority, arrest orders, deportation orders." Benjamin ticked off the charges and the evidence in a monotone. "I think Papon was nothing but a cold and meticulous technician, an agent of organized death. Given the conclusive case against him, I don't understand how he could have had the arrogance to justify himself."

"If you're interested, Mr. Cooker, I have some photocopies of papers he signed while he performed his duties as secretary general of the Gironde prefecture. Most of them are internment orders to the Mérignac camp."

"There was an internment camp at Mérignac?" asked Virgile.

"At the Beaudésert site, at a place called Pichey," Renaud said. "At the corner of the Avenue des Marronniers and the Avenue de l'Hippodrome. After each roundup, Jews, communists, gypsies, and others deemed undesirable were confined to barracks there, in the cold and vermin-filled filth, with no food at all. It was just a half mile as the crow flies from Pey-Berland. Then they were deported. During the time Papon was in charge, more than ten train convoys took deportees to the concentration camp at Drancy near Paris, the last stop before the gas chambers at Auschwitz. Look, here's the list."

Benjamin took the paper and skimmed it before handing it to his assistant, who began to read it aloud.

July 18, 1942, one hundred and sixty-one people; August 26, 1942, four hundred and forty-three people; September 21, 1942, seventy-one people; October 26, 1942, seventy-three; February 2, 1943, one hundred and seven; June 7, 1943, thirty-four; November

25, 1943, ninety-two; December 30, 1943,
one hundred and thirty-six; January 12,
1944, three hundred and seventeen; May
13, 1944, fifty; June 5, 1944, seventy-six.

"I will never look at that city the same way again,
especially when I walk along the platforms at the
Saint Jean train station," Virgile said. His voice
sounded constricted. Benjamin felt sure it was
because of the lump in his throat.

"Getting back to Jules-Ernest Grémillon,"
Benjamin hurriedly interceded, giving Virgile a
moment to collect himself. "Do you know what
role he played in the organizations he belonged to?"

"He didn't have any important duties. He was
pretty much at the bottom of the ladder. He put
up posters and did some security work. He was
an underling. In any case, it doesn't appear that
he was involved in any sordid business, led any
activities, or disseminated propaganda other than
what was on the posters he put up."

"A gofer," Virgile said.

"You got that right. At the time, there was co-
vert fund-raising and some extortion. These organizations needed money, and they often broke
up or became weakened for lack of funds."

"Do you have anything else on him?" Benjamin
asked.

"No, absolutely nothing on Grémillon and
even less on Armand Jouvenaze. That guy is

nowhere to be found. I could find no affiliation with any movement, no evidence that he ever paid membership dues, or any mention of him on attendance lists. His name never appears on the documents I could get my hands on. I do, however, have some information that will be of interest to you regarding Émile Chaussagne. He's in an entirely different category! He was an excellent student at Périgueux High School and a promising law student at the University of Bordeaux until he decided to lend his talents to the French Popular Party and become one of its leaders. He diligently visited the committee room on the Rue Sainte-Catherine and often delivered articles to the movement's two news organizations, sometimes *Le Cri du people,* but especially *L'Assaut,* which had a circulation of barely two thousand but managed to churn out tons of hate-filled propaganda. I have here, as proof, an article from July 18, 1942, which reveals his state of mind. 'It took the June 7 measure ordering Jews to wear the yellow star to get a clear picture of how many inhabit the area. Let's deny Jews access to the main thoroughfares of our city. Deny them access to the trams. Take away their property for the benefit of the bombing victims.'"

"There was already a tramway at that time?" Virgile asked, looking up.

"Yes, even on that point, history is confusing," Benjamin said. He tried to look Renaud in the eye through his thick glasses. "Let's just hope history does not repeat itself! Listening to you, young man, one gets the impression that Bordeaux simply acquiesced to all the grim oppression without attempting any counterforce at all."

"Rest assured, Mr. Cooker, there were also people who rose up against the occupiers, the economic plunder and food shortages, the Milice, the roundups, and the forced labor. You know the people of this region. How could they not react? Spontaneous groups and clandestine networks sprang up, but unfortunately, they were harshly repressed. It's too long a story, but there were leaks, denunciations, and betrayals that undermined the local Resistance movements. I'll spare you the details, but don't forget that the Gestapo played its hand well, and the Resistance fighters in Bordeaux could not hold out. There were also great men in this city's history who acted with dignity. I'm sure you must know the incredible story of Aristide de Sousa Mendès."

Benjamin had never heard of the man. He was surprised, considering the length of time he had lived in the region and his interest in its history. Renaud explained.

"Sousa Mendès was the consul from Portugal," he said. "When the first German convoys arrived in town, there was unbelievable chaos. We have a few pictures of it, notably on the Pont de Pierre, or Stone Bridge, and I guarantee there were never any traffic jams like it, even during construction of the tramway. Everyone was trying to escape, especially the Jews, whether French or Eastern European. There were also stateless people whose nationality was contested or disputed, a hetero-geneous population that didn't have the means to obtain visas. The Portuguese consul's office at 14 Quai Louis-XVIII was under siege, and Sousa Mendès was suddenly faced with an enor-mous moral dilemma. His country was under the thumb of António de Oliveira Salazar. It was an extremely repressive regime. Officially, Portugal was neutral, and Salazar was under orders not to intervene in any occupation activities. Sousa Mendès, however, could not bear the desperate situation of the people who looked to him for help. How could this traditional family man, father of fourteen, and fervent Catholic go against orders that came from a place that was much higher than Salazar—from God Himself?

"Sousa Mendès went off for three days to con-template the terrifying dilemma he faced, and I believe he did a lot of praying. Then, for two weeks, he traveled from Bordeaux and Bayonne to Biarritz and Hendaye. He handed out passes round the clock. He signed and stamped tirelessly, over and over again, without stopping—on the hoods of cars, on suitcases, in makeshift offices, on loose-leaf paper. When there was no paper left, he wrote visas on the pages of magazines and newspapers. He single-handedly saved some thirty thousand Jews. Do you realize? Thirty thousand human beings with only a pen for a weapon!

"His whole life was upended by this decision, which he made freely. He was falsely accused of taking money for the visas he granted. Sousa Mendès died in poverty, forgotten and ostracized by Portuguese society. But he never regretted his acts of disobedience. In 1961, a tree was planted in honor of Sousa Mendès in the Allée des Justes in Jerusalem. But it wasn't until 1994, after years of silence, that a bust and a commemorative plaque were erected in his memory in Bordeaux. And even then, do you know where it is? In the middle of nowhere, in some obscure corner of Mériadeck. He deserved at least to be recognized at the place where he initially resisted: on the banks of the Garonne!"

Renaud's voice remained suspended in heavy silence. To Benjamin, the apartment felt cut off from the rest of the world, isolated behind the thick velour curtains, numb and frozen in time under the dusty chandelier crystals and faded silk embroidery.

"That's a moving story," Benjamin finally murmured. "It reminds me of a simple and enchanting line by the Portuguese poet Fernando Pessoa: "'My head aches, and the universe aches, as well.'"

Before leaving, Benjamin agreed to take a look at Renaud's collection of military paraphernalia in a small area off the living room. Behind the glass cabinets were dozens of medals, gold braids and epaulettes, and ancient arms, some of which were rare pieces from the Napoleonic era. The most impressive specimens seemed to be a medal of merit, the Blue Max, the highest German distinction from the end of the nineteenth century, and a feldgrau, a Prussian officer's uniform. The dark gray of the coat set off the barely intact decorations. Benjamin pretended to admire them while looking repeatedly at his watch. He couldn't stay any longer. When Benjamin and Virgile left the apartment, Renaud was still wearing his raincoat.

8

All Saints Day was approaching, and autumn had finally arrived in Aquitaine. The last hints of summer had been swept away by strong south-westerly winds. The warm air, which had held on until then, had given way to a wet chill that turned the cheeks pink and swelled the fingers. With their coat collars turned up to their ears and their hands plunged deep in their pockets, Benjamin and Virgile stood side by side among the graves in the Libourne cemetery. They were in front of another shattered headstone. Benjamin tried to suppress a sly grin as he pulled a banana out of his Loden. It was hard not to react to Inspector Barbaroux's stupefied look.

"Excuse me," he said as he slowly peeled the fruit. "I am in the middle of a diet, and today I am feasting. I am allowed to have three bananas."

"Go right ahead," the inspector answered. "Don't let me stop you."

"Since this morning, all I've heard about is the black market, hardships, ration cards, and poor people starving to death, and here I am complaining about the low-calorie diet my wife is inflicting on me because I've had the luxury of overindulging for months, if not years."

"Do you really need to diet?" the inspector asked, passing a hand over his paunch.

"So it seems. Too many restaurant meals, not to mention the wines that I must drink because sometimes it's a sin to spit it out. I've put on some pounds."

"I've seen worse."

"Thanks."

"It's true. There wasn't much need for diets during the occupation. It was easy to keep a girlish figure in those days."

"I don't really appreciate your sense of humor, Inspector. I can't bring myself to joke about such things."

"Sorry. I admit I'm not very witty. And yesterday afternoon I wasn't very considerate either. Édouard Prébourg's corpse made me want to puke. But in this line of work, you see so much crap, you have to develop a thick skin. The best way to do that is to joke about it."

"I understand," Benjamin said as he savored the taste and smell of his banana. He sent up an inaudible thank-you for this moment of mercy in his barely tolerable eating regimen. "I brought along my assistant, Virgile Lanssien, who was with me the other day. I hope that's not a problem."

"Not in the least. I assume he's been with you in this business from the beginning."

"Absolutely. He knows about all of it, and I can vouch for his discretion. You know it's one of the golden rules of Cooker & Co." Benjamin fully realized his assistant was catching every word.

"Okay, Mr. Cooker. Let's not beat around the bush. You know exactly what must have happened here. Look at this shit!"

Another grave site had been wrecked, just as Armand Jouvenaze's had been. The white marble plaque, a ceramic wreath, and two black stone vases had been smashed. The headstone was in two pieces. And twelve wine glasses, five of them filled with red wine, had been placed in a semicircle at the edge of the grave. There was also the red paint, but it was more muted. And instead of the word Nazi, there were two angular s's, made to look like lightning strikes. They covered the first letter of the last name:

JEAN SAUVETERRE

1914–1959

"I'm supposed to conclude that this Sauveterre was an SS officer?" Benjamin asked.

"That would be a bit hasty, I think. Maybe he wasn't any more an SS officer than Jouvenaze was a Nazi. We're dealing with a smart aleck who keeps giving us messages and doesn't tell us too much. He wants to keep us intrigued while he goes on wrecking havoc."

"One thing is sure: he can't help committing his murders and desecrations without giving them some meaning."

"Why do you say that? Do you have an idea, perhaps?"

"No more than you do."

"Listen, Mr. Cooker, let's stop playing these idiotic games. I know very well that you've been nosing around at Duboyne de Ladonnet's. You were seen leaving his place just this morning."

"How do you know that? Are you having me followed?"

"It's not worth my time. Who do you take me for?"

"Well then, who told you we met with this young man, who, by the way, is quite a scholar?"

"There are no secrets in Bordeaux. Let's just say that I hear what people say, and gossip keeps doing its thing. At any rate, we're not here at the Libourne cemetery to talk about this."

"Do I have to do another tasting?" Benjamin asked, peering at the sky. It was beginning to darken with clouds.

"No, we don't care. I'll have the samples sent to your office and to your winemaker friend, the famous Depardieu."

"It's Dubourdieu, Inspector," Virgile said.

"It's all the same to me," Barbaroux grumbled. "I tell you, we don't care about this wine. Whether it's a grand cru or a two-buck chuck, it has no bearing!"

"Allow me to have an opinion that's a bit different," Benjamin said.

"Do you have any solid reason to say that?" the inspector asked without waiting for an answer. "Are there any new developments? I want you to know that at this very moment, two of my men are talking to Duboyne de Ladonnet. In a few short hours, their report will be on my desk. I bet they'll find out exactly what you did."

"He had information on the first two victims but nothing at all on Jouvenaze, who is buried nearby," Virgile said. His tone was full of authority. He was letting the inspector know that he was to be taken as seriously as his boss. Benjamin could see that. The captain shot Virgile a surprised and amused look.

"He's a strange fellow, that Duboyne," Barbaroux grumbled as he continued to stare at Virgile.

Now Benjamin was amused. It was clear that the arrogant captain was confronting Virgile, waiting for him to lower his eyes first. Virgile, apparently aware of the inspector's maneuver, refused. Barbaroux finally turned back to Benjamin.

"I've been watching him hang around the city hall archives for quite a while now, interrogating the last people who lived through World War

Two, stirring up stacks of dusty documents. It seems he's trying to prove his grandfather's innocence, although he was embroiled in some dark tale of paintings that were stolen for the Krauts. He's claiming that he wants to honor the memory of his grandfather, but by slaving away on this dossier, he'll end up ruining his maritime insurance company. I don't know how he finds the time to do all that futile research. Wouldn't it look great, the frigging Duboyne de Ladonnet coat of arms, if the heir caused a bankruptcy by screwing around with his grandpa's legacy? He might be a smart guy and a competent historian, but he's just as much of a troublemaker as the rest of them. That was a good idea you had to contact him like that."

"Do you mean that?" Benjamin asked, shocked.

"Do I look like I'm kidding? You have intuition, as we all know, and I have nothing better to do than trail you. But be careful, Mr. Cooker. Don't ever try to hide anything from me again!"

"I hope you didn't have us come here from Bordeaux to give us a lecture or try to intimidate us with unfounded accusations, Inspector."

"Don't be angry. There's nothing threatening in what I'm saying. It's just that it's impossible to sit down calmly with you and discuss our little matter. You seem elusive and not very available. Yesterday you popped in at Édouard Prébourg's place, and then you took off as soon as you finished tasting the wine. You seem to be avoiding me right now. So I might as well meet you informally."

"So, let me get this straight; this new desecration is rather opportune? Do you realize I have a job, too, and duties, urgent matters, employees to manage and pay? I don't imagine your office is sending me a check at the end of the month."

Barbaroux burst out laughing. "You're quite right, Mr. Cooker, because you would be disappointed by the amount."

"Don't be so sure. I find this case very rewarding. And with some luck, we'll eventually reach a settlement."

"You do have a way with words. You always surprise me, Mr. Cooker. Observing you is like being at the theater!"

Benjamin remained stone-faced. He could see Virgile pursing his lips to keep from laughing.

"Ah, there he is, finally!" Barbaroux said when he spied a man walking toward them from a distance. "A good fifteen minutes late, that guy! We've discovered that the two graves are in the same family plot. Jouvenaze and Sauveterre were first cousins. The cemetery office located the only remaining family member in the region. He's Armand's nephew, Dominique Jouvenaze. It's lucky they were able to find him so quickly."

The man was walking slowly. He was wearing a navy pea coat, rust-colored corduroy pants that were too short, and tan work boots. He had an unopened black umbrella slung like a shotgun over his shoulder. The red, green, navy, and yellow tartan scarf around the man's neck was a vivid counterpoint to the otherwise drab look.

Benjamin and Virgile greeted him with a nod and discreetly stepped aside. Benjamin was careful, however, to remain close enough to hear the conversation between the inspector and Arnaud Jouvenaze's nephew.

"Thank you for coming so quickly," Barbaroux said with a smile that looked forced. "I'm sorry for disturbing you, but this is a serious matter."

"You didn't bother me at all, Inspector. I've been retired for two years, so I have all the time in the world."

"Lucky man! At least, that's what they say about retirement."

"Indeed, I didn't expect such a mess when your officer called me this morning. He told me about it."

"Unfortunately, you'll have to file a police report. It's the second grave site in your family that we've found vandalized."

"I read in yesterday's paper that a grave had been desecrated, but since the deceased's name wasn't in the article, I had no idea that it had anything to do with my family. A grave desecration is shocking enough, but that my family was targeted makes it especially upsetting. Will I really have to file a police report?"

"I'll need a statement from you, at least," Barbaroux said. "If we find out who did this, your statement and the report will be essential for any charges we file. Your insurance company will also need what you give us to process your claims and cover the damage. But first, can you tell me about the relationship between the two decedents?"

Dominique Jouvenaze looked fatigued. Benjamin surmised that he was in his late sixties or early seventies, but his slouch made him seem much older. With his tartan scarf pulled up to fend off the chill, he spoke in a monotone. He took his time explaining everything in detail. Jouvenaze gave the appearance of a man who was plumbing the depths of his memory to exhume various pieces of the past.

Jouvenaze told the inspector that his uncle Armand had died of cancer. The illness had dragged on, and he had spent his final days in a Libourne hospital. He was a bachelor his entire life and lived in a modest house. He worked as a farmhand on properties in Pomerol and Lalande de Pomerol. He had acquaintances at a bar in Catusseau, but as far as his nephew knew, the man didn't have any good friends or other close relationships.

The man also admitted that this information was gleaned from what he had been told or had overheard as a child. He had never been allowed to speak to his solitary and taciturn uncle, even though they were neighbors. His parents, Antoine and Simone, both recently deceased, had given him, his brother, and his twin sister strict instructions to never talk to the man. Dominique's parents had much earlier broken off all contact with certain family members.

As for Jean Sauveterre, Jouvenaze had never even met him. He had died in a plane crash in 1959. The DC7 flight from Paris to Abidjan had crashed in a pine forest just outside Bordeaux. It was the biggest plane crash France had ever known. There were fifty-three charred victims, and the blaze had destroyed a good part of the woods.

When the inspector questioned Jouvenaze about the two men's political ties, he said he had no idea why the word Nazi and the SS insignia were left on the tombstones. He had never heard any talk of Nazis or the elite guard when he was growing up, other than what his parents told him about the war. It had to be random graffiti left by some delinquent kids from Libourne, Jouvenaze told the detective.

"All said and done, I'm left to take care of this whole thing, even though these two guys were perfect strangers to me," he wearily concluded. "I have to tell my brother and sister, who live in Paris, and figure out what to do about the graves.

And then there's the matter of Uncle Armand's house, which we inherited when our parents died."

"What do you mean?"

"My father died of a heart attack a year ago, and my mother died three months later. When they inherited Armand's house in 1998, they didn't even open it or put it up for sale. It's been closed since then, and we intend to get rid of it."

"And you've never taken the time to go and look at it?" Barbaroux asked.

"I've been waiting for my brother and sister to come down. This may sound odd to you, but I have qualms about going in there all by myself. My parents pounded it into my siblings and me that we weren't supposed to have anything to do with my uncle. Even now I feel like I'm going against their wishes."

"According to the information I got from the city, it's in the town of Pomerol, right?"

"Yes, in a place called Petite Racine, at the crossroads of Libourne, Pomerol, and Catusseau. It's not very hard to find."

Large drops of rain were beginning to pelt the cemetery. With a handshake, the inspector ended his meeting with Jouvenaze. Benjamin saw the man grimace as he extracted his hand from Barbaroux's grip. The man had an unpleasant handshake. His palm was sweaty, and his grip was strong enough to break fingers. Jouvenaze promised to give his official statement as quickly as possible. He opened his umbrella and started walking away. A few seconds later, a heavy gust of wind ripped through the cemetery, flipping Jouvenaze's umbrella inside out. Virgile shivered and pulled his collar even higher as he watched the man struggle with his umbrella in the distance. When Virgile turned back to the grave, rainwater was running down his forehead. He wiped it dry with the back of his hand.

Benjamin told Barbaroux that he would meet him at his office on the Allées de Tourny the next day, late in the morning, to take stock of the situation. It was time to cross-check the information each one had gathered, compare the viewpoints, and reflect on the mysterious links that seemed to connect the victims. The inspector had suggested that they meet at the restaurant Noailles. When the winemaker reminded him of his cabbage soup diet and offered to share some with the inspector, Barbaroux said a simple meeting over a cup of tea would be just fine. Barbaroux said good-bye and started walking over to his forensics team. The members, who had collected the evidence and taken samples, were waiting for him on a nearby cemetery drive. Just as he was about to reach them, Barbaroux turned around. He ran back to Benjamin and grabbed his arm.

"Say, Cooker, about that tea. Could we make it a little Armagnac instead?"

9

Before returning to Bordeaux to complete the final stage of the Languedoc-Roussillon tasting, Benjamin Cooker could not resist the urge to walk the grounds of Pomerol with his assistant, if only for a half hour squeezed out of his tight schedule. He often indulged in this type of escape. He always had an irrepressible desire to smell the vines that bore the fruit of a highly regarded wine.

They drove aimlessly, letting themselves be guided by signposts that inspired wine lovers to daydream: Bellegrave, Beauregard, Le Bon Pasteur, Bourgneuf-Vayron, Le Castellet, Clos de Salles, La Conseillante, La Croix Saint-Georges, Domaine de l'Église, L'Enclos, Franc-Maillet, Gazin, Gombaude-Guillot, Grand Beauséjour, Grand Moulinet, Latour à Pomerol, Montviel, Petit Village, Pomeaux, Ratouin, Rouget, Tour Maillet, Tour Robert, Trotanoy, Vieux Château Certan, Vieux Maillet, Vray Croix de Gay. The road wound its way slowly between the vineyards. The châteaux blended with the countryside in soft, peaceful harmony to the metronome of the swishing windshield wipers.

"I've never been to the Pétrus château, boss."

"You don't just drop in for a visit, my boy. There are certain sacred places you are rarely allowed to enter. I won't take you there today, out of consideration for the people who work there. I wouldn't want to disturb them by arriving without an appointment. But I promise you'll make a pilgrimage there someday."

"Do you know that I have never even tasted Pétrus?" Virgile admitted.

"That's a gaping hole in your estimable expertise," Benjamin joked. "We'll have to correct it as soon as possible. I'm sure you know that one of the most distinctive characteristics of the Pomerol appellation is its geological composition. The earth is full of fairly fine, lovely gravel, but it's especially the *crasse de fer,* or iron dross, that gives it its uniqueness.

"Yes, I didn't study oenology at the university for nothing. The *crasse de fer* is in the subsoil, which is a stony mix of clay and iron. The iron oxide gives the wine its metallic but fatty flavor. Some people claim it tastes a bit like truffles."

"Perfect. Young man, you've learned your lessons well. But you know, it just so happens that the twenty-eight acres of Pétrus are composed solely of clay and silty sand. And therein lies the whole mystery. There is no *crasse de fer* in the

Pétrus domain, whiles it's the main element influencing all the Pomerols. If you open a map of that appellation, you'll see this little yellow spot right in the middle of the terroir. Perfect and unique, as if the finger of God had pointed to this precise place and blessed it. Do you understand what I'm trying to say?"

"Sort of," Virgile murmured. Knowing his assistant as he did, Benjamin could sense his skepticism.

"God marked the spot. Then He lifted his finger, and Pétrus was born, steeped in holy clay! But perhaps I digress. You don't seem very convinced by my theory."

"It's quite tempting, sir, though I find it a bit too mystical for my taste. I would advise you to keep it to yourself and not let it slip into one of your books. Some people might brand you a theo-oenologist—to coin a term—and that would be unfortunate. You would be forced to drink only consecrated wine to the end of your days! And we both know how awful that tends to be."

"You're right. I agree. People don't always realize the divine nature of what they're drinking."

The rain had almost stopped by the time they reached the Pomerol church, where the bell tower rose up like a lighthouse in a sea of vineyards. They parked the convertible on the small town square and walked over to the war memorial. Benjamin read the names of the soldiers who had died in battle. Pomerol had lost thirty-one men in World War One. Five young men had been lost from 1939 to 1945. Benjamin bowed his head and remained silent, arms crossed and eyes half closed. He prayed for the souls of the boys who had died far from home and the mothers, fathers, and siblings who had lost them. As he sent up his prayers, he could hear the birds chirping in the vines.

Benjamin opened his eyes and saw his assistant waiting patiently. He took in the landscape and noted that there weren't many leaves left in the vineyards, just a few reddish bouquets hanging here and there on the stocks, dozing before the first winter pruning.

"There's something I have to tell you, sir," Virgile said. "But I'm not sure if I'm right or wrong or if I should just trust my intuition. Besides, it was so brief and fleeting. A little while ago, in the cemetery…"

"How cautious you're being, Virgile!"

"Well, here it is: I think I saw streaks of red on Dominique Jouvenaze's umbrella. Not while it was closed, but as soon as it started to rain, the guy opened it, and there, on the cloth part, near the top, there were red smears. It looked like paint, and it was bright red, like an intense vermilion."

"And then?"

"Well, while you were talking with the inspector, I watched him. He was fighting with the umbrella in the wind, and at one point, the umbrella even inverted. I got a good look at it. When I turned back to the grave and saw the two *s*'s, they looked like they were the same red."

"What are you trying to say?"

"Nothing, I'm just telling you what I saw. Or what I think I saw."

Jangling the keys to the Mercedes, Benjamin walked back to the car with Virgile. Without a word, he slid behind the wheel. They took off in the direction of the primary school, turned left toward Catusseau, and crossed a highway. They drove along narrow roads that were rough enough to make the car shake. Near a tributary of the L'Isle River, not far from the railroad tracks connecting Bordeaux to Bergerac, was the place called Petite Racine. Barely a handful of modest houses were set among the vines and protected from the wind by oak, sycamore, and acacia trees. Only a beautiful nineteenth-century monastery surrounded by conifers and a stone wall gave character to the uninspired hamlet. Benjamin cut the engine after parking in a secluded spot near an overrun thicket.

As soon as Benjamin got out of the car, he faced into the wind to attune his sense of smell to the landscape. Oddly, it was a habit he had picked up from his Irish setter, Bacchus. Then, standing still, he got his visual bearings. He assessed the way the rows of vines were established and the nature of the soil, more gravelly than sandy in this place. Nearby would be the Marzy château. Toward the west would be La Croix des Templiers. Behind him was La Pointe.

It did not take Benjamin and Virgile long to locate Armand Jouvenaze's house near a large pond. In the distance, the nephew's house was visible. It was slightly more imposing but just as plain. Plumes of smoke escaped in thin threads from the large brick chimney, indicating that Dominique Jouvenaze was home. A barrier of trees separated the two properties. Benjamin and Virgile cautiously snooped around the little house. Its closed shutters and deserted courtyard overrun with high weeds typified the morbid nature of neglected properties. Virgile walked over to the barn, its worn siding bleached by years of scorching sun and pounded by relentless rains. He motioned to Benjamin to join him.

"Look, boss. I think you're going to like this."

Benjamin peeked through a space in the wood and whistled. "That's for sure!"

"What model is it?"

"A Renault Dauphine, my boy! In pretty good condition, from what I can tell. A magnificent red Dauphine!"

"Not as cool as my Peugeot 403."

"I grant you that, but seeing this Dauphine was worth the trip!"

Benjamin told his assistant about his meeting with Alain Massip. A man named Armand had come to the leather shop regularly to pick up Jules-Ernest Grémillon and take him to the pool hall in Mériadeck.

"Shit! You think it's the same car?"

"It's quite a coincidence, don't you think?"

"I must admit, this business is beginning to get interesting," Virgile said, rubbing his hands together.

"The ideal thing would be getting into the old man's house and seeing what's inside," Benjamin said.

"It's tempting, but how would we do that? The only way I see is crawling in through the coal shoot in the cellar. Look over there, in the foundation."

"That's not a bad idea, my boy! In fact, that's very clever, especially since the lock on the shoot doesn't look all that strong."

"It does look like it could be broken fairly easily. Maybe the car jack for the Dauphine would do the trick."

"Why not give it a try? No forced entry through the front door, no shutters pulled open or windows broken. The coal shoot seems to be a perfect way to get into the house."

"That's right, boss. No one would know the difference."

"Yes, it's tempting, but still rather risky. Let's not hang around. In a half hour, we have to be in the lab to begin tasting the Corbières. We absolutely have to make up for lost time, and if we really push it, we can even knock off all the notes on the slopes of Vérargues, Saint-Christol, and La Clape."

"You're not going to tell Barbaroux?" Virgile asked. Benjamin could read the disappointment in his assistant's face.

"I'll see him tomorrow. There will be plenty of time to tell him about it."

They made the drive back to Bordeaux in record time, and as soon as they arrived at the laboratory on the Cours du Chapeau-Rouge, they went straight to work. As usual, Alexandrine de la Palussière had carefully prepared the tasting. She was surprised that they were late, because they were usually on time, if not early. But she asked no questions and let them concentrate on the sleeved bottles. When she left at the end of the afternoon, they were still taking notes, and several dozen bottles waited on the white-tile lab counter for their verdict. They completed the entire assignment and left the laboratory at eleven forty-five. Benjamin suggested grabbing a quick dinner at the Régent, where service often ran late into the night.

"What about your diet, sir?"

"No problem. Tomorrow is the fifth day, and I am allowed ten to twenty ounces of grilled lean beef, as well as six fresh tomatoes. And tomorrow is in fifteen minutes; I'll just start the day a little early."

"If you look at it that way."

The meal arrived quickly. Benjamin looked appreciatively at his allotted portion of meat, along with the two tomatoes cut into quarters without any seasoning. He noted the little decorative basil leaf and nibbled with satisfaction, pleased with this esthetic accompaniment that spiced up the Spartan simplicity of the dish. Virgile, meanwhile, plunged his fork into a duck confit gratin that he washed down with two glasses of Côtes-de-Bourg. When they were back on the sidewalk of the Place Gambetta, Benjamin gave his assistant the keys to his convertible.

"How would you like to take a little drive to Pomerol?"

"Right now?" Virgile asked, visibly taken aback.

"I don't think we'll be able to sleep if we don't verify certain things."

"Speak for yourself, boss. I'm beat."

"Come on, buck up! I'm sure you haven't been able to stop thinking about it, either."

"Yes, but still... At this hour?"

"Exactly, it will be perfect. We weren't going to break into Uncle Armand's little shack in broad daylight, were we?"

"And what if we get caught? It doesn't matter if it's day or night."

"We'll think about that later. You must admit, it's exciting, this little after-dinner gambit!"

"Okay, but promise me we'll make it quick. We'll stay just long enough to take a look."

Virgile drove with a heavy foot, and the Bordeaux to Libourne trip set a new record. Benjamin held onto his seat the entire way. They did not slow down until they reached Catusseau and arrived at the edge of Petite Racine. Despite the darkness, they found their way to Armand Jouvenaze's house. They pushed open the barn door and found the car jack in the trunk of the Dauphine. The lock on the coal hatch gave way with a clean snap, and despite their heavy coats, they slipped easily through the opening.

"Finally, the diet is paying off," Virgile said. "Only a week ago, I would have had to push you through."

"Don't try to be funny, Virgile. You'll see when you're my age how easily you can put on weight and how hard it is to take it off."

The cellar had a low ceiling, which forced them to stoop. Benjamin lit his lighter and swept the flame around him to get a good view of the space. The walls were seeping moisture. A few lumps of coal were strewn in the corner. An old tin watering can, half-decayed hemp ropes, a container of motor oil, and rusty mousetraps completed the scene. Along one wall, they spotted a door and pushed it open. Its mournful creak almost made

Benjamin jump. Inside this smaller cellar room, metal racks held several bottles on their sides. Their colors danced in the glow of the lighter. Benjamin and Virgile blew the dust off the labels: two Château Cantelauzes, three Clos Renés, a Château Lafleur, and four Château Bassonneries, just to name the Pomerol appellations. The rest bore Côtes de Castillon, Bourg, and Blaye labels. There were also a pair of Listracs and ten bottles of generic Bordeaux.

"Not a single Pétrus, boss!"

"It was too good to be true," Benjamin said, shrugging.

"Yep, our hopes were too high," his assistant said with a sigh.

Benjamin was about to suggest that they leave when something caught his eye. He had moved the flame just a few inches, and that was enough to illuminate a set of parallel grooves in the dirt floor. Virgile quickly saw what he had just spotted.

"Look over here!" Virgile exclaimed. "On the ground! And over there! And here, too!"

"Don't talk so loud, Virgile," Benjamin said, squatting to get a closer look at the tracks. It looks to me like crates were dragged right across the floor."

"In my opinion, boss, they were full, or they wouldn't have left such deep grooves. At any rate, with these low ceilings it wouldn't be possible to move a crate of wine any other way."

"I agree. That's the only thing it could be. And if you look closer, you can see where the crates were originally. They were next to this rack. It's possible that one of the crates could have held a dozen bottles."

"One thing is for sure: the grooves are fresh."

"Yes, and it's time to go to bed. Tomorrow is another day!"

10

"They just bumped off another one, Mr. Cooker."

They were talking on their cell phones, and Benjamin could hear the exhaustion and exasperation in the inspector's voice. As usual, it also contained a note of belligerence. When Benjamin didn't reply, Barbaroux raised his voice even more. Now his delivery was strident.

"Élie Péricaille, eighty-nine years old. He tried to defend himself, and I can't even begin to describe the carnage. Blood up to the ceiling! And the smell. You don't want to know. The guys in the lab say he must have been rotting for three or four days."

Benjamin still said nothing.

"I'm in deep shit, Mr. Cooker. Half the glasses are now full. Hello, are you there?"

"It all depends on how you look at it, Inspector. You could also say that half the glasses are still empty, fortunately."

"That's just like you, putting that kind of spin on it," Barbaroux said. His voice wasn't quite as loud. Benjamin guessed that he was trying to collect himself. "We were scheduled to meet later this morning, but would you mind if I came over now? Actually, I'm here already."

"Do I really have a choice? Come on up. I'm here."

When Barbaroux walked into the office, a tulip glass filled with Armagnac awaited him on the leather desk blotter. The winemaker was sipping Grand Yunnan in a porcelain cup in the colors of the Grand Dukedom of Kent, royal blue, scarlet, and gold.

"Okay, all cards on the table!" the inspector said. "Who's going to start?"

Benjamin took a sip of tea and smacked his lips.

"You go, detective. For once, the English won't fire first."

"As you like." Barbaroux smiled. "First of all, I have to tell you that little Duboyne de Ladonnet was terrific with the two detectives I sent over. He confirmed what we already knew about Grémillon and Chaussagne and their political activities during the occupation. In fact, he knows more about it than our intelligence services, and that's saying something!"

"As far as Édouard Prébourg, the third victim, is concerned, I assume you also went looking for information on his wartime activities?"

"His trail was much easier to follow. He did jail time, and intelligence had information on him, primarily because of his ties with the facist Falange movement after the occupation. Later, he became involved in one crooked scheme after another: pimping, fraud, bank robbery. At that time, he was crashing in the old Mériadeck neighborhood and had teamed with the infamous Albert Bitrian, who was calling the shots in the slums of Bordeaux. A bloody bastard, that Bitrian! Strip joints, illegal gambling, extortion, a bit of opium in the whorehouses down by the port, and all the hoodlums in the city kissing up to him. You didn't want to piss off the Bull."

"What did you say? The Bull?"

"Yes, that's what they called him, because he had a tendency to see red when he came across a communist. And incidentally, the Gestapo didn't mind using his henchmen when they needed to bust up the Resistance fighters. The most surprising thing is how he made out after the liberation. He must have accommodated everybody, because no one bothered him. It's the same old story with most of the big shots in the area. Okay, I've given you my basic facts. Now it's your turn."

Benjamin put down his teacup. "What a coincidence. I have also heard of the Bull."

"Is that so?"

"Yes, Alain Massip remembered this man when I asked him about Jules-Ernest Grémillon. It seems he often went to a billiard hall with friends, and a certain Armand used to come by the shop and pick him up in a red Renault Dauphine, along with someone nicknamed the Bull. Why are you smiling like that, Inspector?"

"Go on, please. I'll tell you later."

"Virgile and I went for a walk in Petite Racine, and…"

"And?"

"And we found what I believe is this Dauphine. It's in a garage belonging to the deceased Jouvenaze. That must be the fellow named Armand who used to come by and pick up Grémillon."

"Very good, Mr. Cooker! I was smiling because we have found something interesting too: a membership roster for a nonprofit organization dating from the early nineteen fifties. All of our shady characters are listed as members of the French Billiard Club, which often met at Chez Joseph, a bar in Mériadeck. It was protected by Bitrian's goons. A guy named Joseph Larède owned the place. He flirted with various fascist movements during the war, especially the Legion of French Volunteers. Their meeting place was right next door to this building, at 28 Allées de Tourny. A lot of them were degenerates who wanted to go to Russia and fight Bolshevism. Joseph Larède dropped out and became involved in the black market. He got in trouble after the war for smuggling sardines and whisky. He died in 1968, certainly not before seeing the barricades and student demonstrations all over Paris. He must have died of anger. Serves him right!"

"But I haven't told you everything, Inspector," Benjamin said, a bit uneasy. "I have a little revelation for you, which will require a bit of indulgence on your part."

"You've used some slightly unorthodox methods in your investigation, and you don't want to get into any trouble, I suppose?" Barbaroux was wearing an amused smile.

"Exactly."

"Go on. I promise that when I leave here I will have seen nothing and heard nothing."

"We went snooping in Armand Jouvenaze's house. Well, just the cellar, and we discovered some very disturbing evidence."

The winemaker recounted the nocturnal escapade. The captain twirled his tulip glass on the leather desk blotter as he listened.

"Mr. Cooker, I have one word to say to you: bravo! You may have put your finger on the one point that's been gnawing at me from the beginning of this investigation."

"The repeated use of Pétrus wine in these hateful acts frustrates me too. What a waste of the best merlots in creation! It's a sin, pouring that nectar in the presence of such lowlifes. This distresses me even more because it sullies the reputation of Pétrus: a round, supple, rich, charming, joyful, elegant, and vigorous wine. It's a wine of peace and generosity."

"That's all very nice, but we have to find out why the wine plays a part in each of these crimes. Where are these fucking bottles, and why are they so important to the murderer? The answer is definitely at the bottom of the cellar, don't you agree?"

"I hope you're right, Inspector. By the way, I have a story to tell you. I don't know if it's true or if it's in the diocesan archives, but they say that one day the bishop of Bordeaux paid a visit to one of his abbots and reprimanded him just before he left. 'Father, I am disturbed by all the spirits in your cellar.' The priest calmly answered, 'Put your mind at ease, Monsignor. They all saw the priest before they died.'"

"That's a good one." Barbaroux laughed. "If you don't mind, I'm going to steal it. I know some friends who would enjoy it."

"Go ahead. You have my permission."

Barbaroux left Benjamin's office after telling him that he would investigate the French Billiard Club. As it turned out, the club had never had more than twelve members, and the list had not changed for two decades. Jules-Ernest Grémillon, Émile Chaussagne, Armand Jouvenaze, Jean Sauveterre, Édouard Prébourg, Albert Bitrian, and Joseph Larède were all part of the group, as well as the latest victim, Élie Péricaille, who had also been a particularly sadistic member of

Milice. This left only four more names: Gabriel Bergerive, Gustave Tasdori, Arthur Darnaudon, and Edmond Cosinac. These men were still living, and they were given protection. Only one still lived on his own. The others were in nursing homes between Langon and Mont-de-Marsen.

Barbaroux called Benjamin the next day to tell him that he had obtained search warrants for the home of the deceased Armand Jouvenaze, as well as that of his nephew. He told Benjamin that he and Virgile could accompany the police as wine experts. He just asked that they keep their distance from the search and become involved only if bottles of Pétrus were found.

Police cars raced to Petite Racine, their lights flashing and their sirens blaring. When the officers arrived at Dominique Jouvenaze's home to get the keys to Uncle Armand's house, no one answered the door. A locksmith was called to open old Jouvenaze's door, and the rooms were searched from top to bottom. Pictures were taken in the cellar, where a technician took plaster impressions of the grooves running across the dirt floor. After an hour of painstaking and unceremonious searching, they could only conclude that there was no bottle in the cellar that would shed any light on the investigation.

Barbaroux went back to Dominique Jouvenaze's house and pounded on the door for more than a quarter of an hour, to no avail. The locksmith was called upon once more, and he eventually managed to release the bolt.

When the door gave way, two detectives burst into the house, their guns drawn. But no one put up any resistance. In the kitchen, a purple-faced Dominique Jouvenaze was swinging from the exposed beam. It took three men to get the writhing man down. It was too late. Lying on the tiled floor, Dominique Jouvenaze died in a final gasp.

Under the sink, the detectives found two cases of Pétrus. Only one was open. The inspector pulled it out and passed it to Benjamin, who picked up one of the bottles. Saint Peter, holding the keys to paradise, stared indulgently at the winemaker, his face barely obscured by the dust shrouding the black and bloodred label distinctly marked 1942.

The windows were open, but the house still smelled of mildew and urine. On the plastic floral tablecloth, a handwritten letter quivered in the breeze.

11

My dear child,

By the time you read this letter, I will be gone. I know that I often annoyed you with my advice and petty obsessions. Do you remember that tartan scarf that you never wanted to wear to school? We played a little game every day when it was cold outside. I would pull it up around your ears in the morning. And in the afternoon, when you came home, I would find it at the bottom of your schoolbag. I just wanted you to be warm, and you were afraid you would look silly in front of your friends.

Pardon my handwriting. It's so unsteady. But it is not so much my hands that hurt or the fact that I'm getting weaker and weaker. I'm trembling because I barely have the courage to tell you so many things that I should have told you long before I became so frail. Pain and sickness are nothing, compared to what I have needed to reveal for so long. How many times did I try? How many times did I change my mind and back down? God forgive me for lying out of fear, cowardice, and the prospect of losing you! I spent my life lying to you, your brother, your sister, even myself. Your father was the only one who understood my dread, but you know how sweet and thoughtful he was, and in the end, he was as fearful and weak as I have been.

Today I know it's time to talk to you about yourself, finally. Before you read the rest of this letter, go and find a chair to sit in and take a deep breath.

Your real name is Samuel Frydman, and you are the son of Isaac and Irma Frydman. I knew your real parents, and when they asked me to take you in, I was very honored to help them. Your father was a man who commanded respect as soon as he spoke. He was a professor at the law school in Paris, and he met your mother at a concert at the Salle Pleyel. She was young—ten years younger than Samuel—but she was wise beyond her years. I saw some pictures of her at that time in her life, and she looked very distinguished, which is better than beautiful. Her family lived in Warsaw, but she left everything to be with your father in France. She even left behind her career as a pianist and all the hopes everyone had for her.

I didn't know them very well. Our conversations were often too brief, but they had handsome faces and beautiful blue eyes. Yours are the only blue eyes we have ever had in the Jouvenaze family. It was Dr. Capderoque, the doctor from Libourne and a good friend of your father's, who took them in and hid them in the abandoned monastery at the intersection leading to Petite Racine. This man was good and generous. He listened only to his heart when he decided to protect Jews no one else would help. It was 1942, and I realize now that he was naïve, as well as good and generous. Dr. Capderoque thought his status and influence, his Catholic faith, and the good will of his many acquaintances were enough to save an entire family. For two years, Isaac, Irma, your brother, Simon, and your sister, Sarah, lived behind closed shutters in fear of being discovered. They even went without heat in the winter, because they feared someone would see smoke coming out of the chimney.

The doctor trusted us enough to ask us to help these poor people. Under the pretext of airing out the monastery, I was able to help your parents by bringing them hot meals, taking care of their laundry, and keeping them in supplies. Your father (I'm talking about Antoine, my husband, because it's hard not to think of him as your dad) helped me enormously.

Once a month, the doctor would spend the weekend at the monastery. He told people that he was doing light maintenance on the grounds. What he was really doing was bringing books to the family and generally looking after them.

Irma became pregnant in the spring of 1943, just as I did. We were both very proud of our big bellies. We wondered which of us would give birth first. You were born November 17, eight days before your sister Madeleine. Irma's pregnancy was more difficult than mine. I'm sure her anxiety over giving birth in secret played a part. The fact is, she could have died if Antoine hadn't gone by bicycle to Libourne to get the good doctor. She came out of it very weak and didn't have enough milk to nurse you. You were beginning to waste away, and we were all terribly worried.

Luckily, I had given birth to your sister at exactly twelve fifteen on November 25, and Antoine, without asking me, went to get you at the monastery. When your little hands grabbed my breast, I knew there would be enough milk for two babies. Irma was heartbroken but also relieved. She knew you would be saved. With your parents' consent, we went to the city hall and registered you as our own son. That is how you and Madeleine became twins.

In January 1944, during the nights of the tenth and the eleventh, there was a big roundup, and we found out through Dr. Capderoque that two hundred and twenty-eight Jews, both adults and children, had been confined to a synagogue in Bordeaux and then sent to Drancy in cattle cars. The train stopped at the Libourne station to transport other Jews who had been arrested in the region, as well as Blaye.

We paid even more attention to our every movement between the house and the monastery. We had to be guarded around everyone and heighten our vigilance. Irma was doing a little better, despite the terrible winter that year. I don't know, and we will never know, how Armand discovered that your family was there. I never felt close to my brother-in-law, but I couldn't imagine that he would be that soulless to have any part in what happened next. When he and his friends got to the monastery, they were already drunk. I never understood why he started going to that billiard club. People in the area said it was owned by a collaborationist, and all sorts of informers and black-market traffickers from Bordeaux frequented the place. What could have come over him that he would wallow among such swine?

I would rather not tell you exactly what they did to your family. I've had too many nightmares. Just know that your father was killed with a knife while trying to defend his family. Irma, Simon, and Sarah were sent to the Mérignac camp before being shipped to Auschwitz on the convoy of May 13, 1944. They never returned.

Your family's other executioners were Jules-Ernest Grémillon, Émile Chaussagne, Gabriel Bergerive, Édouard Prébourg, Gustave Tasdori, Jean Sauveterre, Arthur Darnaudon, Élie

Péricaille, Joseph Larède, Albert Bitrian, and Edmond Cosinac.

I don't know which one of them held the knife that killed your father, but they are all guilty of exterminating your family. Now you know why I never had anything to do with Armand. You can only imagine the depth of his darkness when I tell you that we saw him prowling around the monastery the day after the crime. We watched him carry out several cases of wine. I believe Dr. Capderoque kept them stored there. That good man had already been arrested and shot.

I think Armand might have had some suspicions about you. Every day I sensed him spying on us from behind his curtains, and I was always on edge when I saw him watching you playing near the barn or in the yard. I was afraid that your eyes would give you away. But I believe that Armand, as depraved as he was, could not turn in his own brother's family. Likewise, your father didn't have the heart to turn in his brother after the liberation. So we ignored one another, although it wasn't easy having him so close.

When he died, we inherited his house, of course. There weren't many people at the burial, just a few friends, I was told. I never wanted to set foot in his house, and neither did your father.

So now you know. They are just names on a piece of paper, and they are not worthy of being called men. Maybe they are dead today. Who knows what became of them, what fate had in store for them? Whatever you do, do not try to find them. I know you. There is no point seeking revenge after all these years. I am sure their lives have been miserable, and one day or another they will pay for their crimes, if they haven't already.

Although there's not a day that I don't grieve for the mother who brought you into the world, I thank God for the privilege of raising you as my son. I have loved you with every fiber of my being. Maybe when you were little, you thought I loved you too much. But now you understand how fiercely I wanted to protect you.

Take care of yourself, my love, and when you wrap that scarf around your neck, remember me.

Your mother, in spite of everything.

EPILOGUE

Seated at the back of the Gravelier restaurant, Benjamin Cooker and Virgile Lanssien ordered a bottle of Pomerol, Château Beauregard, 2000. After enjoying some appetizers of salmon in puff pastry, they greedily devoured their entrées. Virgile feasted on a sea scallop fricassee with spinach in a lemon cream sauce, while Benjamin was happy with a rabbit confit embellished with prawns and a blood-orange sauce.

When the dishes arrived, the bottle was almost empty, and they agreed to be unfaithful to their native territory and treat themselves to the caress of a Savigny-Lès-Beaune, La Dominode, a premier cru from Pavelot. They had both chosen the same main course: pigeon served with fried liver, bean sprouts, and grilled carrots, which they ate without exchanging a word.

Virgile did not order dessert and opted for a very strong coffee instead. Benjamin could not resist the promise of a dessert in the form of a cigar: a sweetly oily Cuba Libre with hints of dark chocolate. The winemaker poured himself another glass of Burgundy, discreetly loosened his belt, relaxed his stomach muscles, sank deeper into the cushioned bench seat, and rolled the cigar between his fingers.

A sad smile came across his lips.

In a single evening, Benjamin Cooker had certainly gained back half the weight he had lost on his seven-day cabbage-soup diet.

Thank you for reading Deadly Tasting.

We invite you to share your thoughts and reactions on Goodreads and your favorite social media and retail platforms.

We appreciate your support.

The Winemaker Detective Series

A total epicurean immersion in French countryside and gourmet attitude with two expert winemakers turned amateur sleuths gumshoeing around wine country. The following titles are currently available in English.

Treachery in Bordeaux

The start of this wine plus crime mystery series, this journey to Bordeaux takes readers behind the scenes of a grand cru wine estate that has fallen victim to either negligence or sabotage. Winemaker turned gentleman detective Benjamin Cooker sets out to find out what happened and why. Who would want to target this esteemed estate?

www.treacheryinbordeaux.com

Grand Cru Heist

In another epicurean journey in France, wine critic Benjamin Cooker's world gets turned upside down one night in Paris. He retreats to the region around Tours to recover. There, a flamboyant British dandy, a spectacular blue-eyed blonde, a zealous concierge, and touchy local police disturb his well-deserved rest. From the Loire Valley to Bordeaux, in between a glass of Vouvray and a bottle of Saint-Émilion, the Winemaker Detective and his assistant Virgile turn PI to solve two murders and a very particular heist. Who stole those bottles of grand cru classé?

Nightmare in Burgundy

In this one, the Winemaker Detective leaves his native Bordeaux to go to Burgundy for a dream wine-tasting trip to France's other key wine-making region. Between Beaune, Dijon and Nuits-Saint-Georges, the excursion becomes a nightmare when he stumbles upon a mystery revolving around messages from another era. What do they mean? What dark secrets from the deep past are haunting the Clos de Vougeot? Does blood need to spill to sharpen people's memory?

www.nightmareinburgundy.com

ABOUT THE AUTHORS

Noël Balen (left) and Jean-Pierre Alaux (right).
(©David Nakache)

Jean-Pierre Alaux and **Noël Balen** came up with the Winemaker Detective over a glass of wine, of course. Jean-Pierre Alaux is a magazine, radio, and television journalist when he is not writing novels in southwestern France. He is a genuine wine and food lover, and won the Antonin Carême prize for his cookbook *La Truffe sur le Soufflé*, which he wrote with the chef Alexis Pélissou. He is the grandson of a winemaker and exhibits a real passion for wine and winemaking. For him, there is no greater common denominator than wine. Coauthor of the series Noël Balen lives in Paris, where he shares his time between writing, making records, and lecturing on music. He plays bass, is a music critic, and has authored a number of books about musicians, in addition to his novel and short-story writing.

ABOUT THE TRANSLATOR

Sally Pane studied French at State University of New York Oswego and the Sorbonne before receiving her master's degree in French literature from the University of Colorado, where she wrote *Camus and the Americas: A Thematic Analysis of Three Works Based on His Journaux de Voyage.* Her career includes more than twenty years of translating and teaching French and Italian at Berlitz and at Colorado University Boulder. She has worked in scientific, legal, and literary translation; her literary translations include *Operatic Arias; Singers Edition,* and *Reality and the Untheorizable* by Clément Rosset. She also served as the interpreter for the government cabinet of Rwanda and translated for Dian Fossey's Digit Fund. In addition to her passion for French, she has studied Italian at Colorado University, in Rome and in Siena. She lives in Boulder, Colorado, with her husband.

Discover more books from

Le French Book

www.lefrenchbook.com

The 7th Woman by Frédérique Molay

An edge-of-your-seat mystery set in Paris, where beautiful sounding names surround ugly crimes that have Chief of Police Nico Sirsky and his team on tenterhooks.

www.the7thwoman.com

The Paris Lawyer by Sylvie Granotier

A psychological thriller set between the sophisticated corridors of Paris and a small backwater in central France, where rolling hills and quiet country life hide dark secrets.

www.theparislawyer.com

The Greenland Breach by Bernard Besson

The Arctic ice caps are breaking up. Europe and the East Coast of the United States brace for a tidal wave. A team of freelance spies face a merciless war for control of discoveries that will change the future of humanity.

www.thegreenlandbreach.com

The Bleiberg Project by David Khara

Are Hitler's atrocities really over? Find out in this adrenaline-pumping ride to save the world from a conspiracy straight out of the darkest hours of history.

www.thebleibergproject.com

CPSIA information can be obtained at www.ICGtesting.com
Printed in the USA
BVOW04s1636170914

367256BV00003B/5/P

9 781939 474216